POLKA DOT DREAMS

Natty loves vintage clothes and fabulous fifties music, so she thinks she's found her perfect man when she meets Matt, who runs a rock 'n' roll themed ice-cream parlour. However, Matt's life is rather complicated — will Cameron, the mysterious Scottish Teddy Boy promising to make her a singing star, turn Natty's head? Natty finds an ally in Matt's mum, Margie, a seaside landlady, but can she really find an old-fashioned love in this rock 'n' roll romance?

JULIA DOUGLAS

POLKA DOT DREAMS

Complete and Unabridged

LINFORD
Leicester

First published in Great Britain in 2012

First Linford Edition
published 2013

British Library CIP Data

Douglas, Julia.
  Polka dot dreams. - -
  (Linford romance library)
  1. Love stories.
  2. Large type books.
  I. Title II. Series
  823.9'2–dc23

  ISBN 978–1–4448–1466–8

Published by
F. A. Thorpe (Publishing)
Anstey, Leicestershire

Set by Words & Graphics Ltd.
Anstey, Leicestershire
Printed and bound in Great Britain by
T. J. International Ltd., Padstow, Cornwall

This book is printed on acid-free paper

1

Natty trotted across the station concourse as quickly as she could, considering that she was wearing vintage three-inch stilettos finished in red velvet with a white polka dot toe; a tight-at-the-knee, genuine 1950s pencil dress in violet satin beneath a swirling leopardskin coat trimmed with chocolate brown fur; and carrying a trunk-sized suitcase in one hand and a guitar case in the other.

To the other commuters criss-crossing the cavernous and echoing London terminus, Natty looked as if she'd fallen through a time-warp from the golden age of Hollywood, or perhaps wandered in from a musical on the West End stage.

Her ruby-red hair was rolled up into a bulbous pompadour at the front and swept back at the sides to bounce in three rows of carefully rolled curls on

1

her slim, fur-trimmed shoulders. The fiery hue of her locks was complemented by an orange orchid pinned above her left ear. Her smoke-coloured stockings were seamed with a black pinstripe and her make-up was red-carpet-ready, from her delicately plucked and pencilled eyebrows and long false eyelashes to the precision-applied beauty spot to the top left of her scarlet Cupid's-bow lips.

Ordinarily, Natty would have relished the attention, all the heads turning her way in admiration or curiosity. She loved bringing a bit of colour and retro glamour into the drab reality of everyday life. The smiles that tended to greet her wherever she went made her daily efforts with powder, pins, brushes and tongs worthwhile.

Amid the bustling travellers, distorted train announcements and flying pigeons of the railway station, she might, on another occasion, have found time to enjoy a little fantasy that she was starring in the final dramatic scene of a classic black-and-white weepie — a tragic heroine fleeing a doomed romance.

But for once Natty had no time to have her head in the clouds. She really was a girl on the run. And as her scarlet heels click-clacked on the tiled concourse, only one thought went through Natty's mind: *I'd better not miss that train!*

As the destination board clattered high above the concourse, the ticket collector was closing the platform gate.

'Wait for me!' Natty trilled. Realising her ticket wasn't to hand, she set down her cases and reached with kid-gloved hands for the gold clasp of her white heart-shaped handbag.

'Don't worry about it, love.' The ticket man waved her through the gate. 'Just get a move on or you'll miss your train. Mmmm. Nice perfume,' he added as she swept by.

The guard had a whistle in his mouth, but refrained from blowing it until he'd opened the door of the last carriage for her.

'Mind the step, Miss.' The youth eyed the flash of her stockinged calves and a figure shaped like an hourglass by the forgotten secrets of a 1950s girdle and bullet bra. For Natty, there was no stinting behind the scenes — a period-perfect silhouette meant the right foundations.

A moment later, the whistle blew, the diesel rumbled, the carriage lurched and the train began to roll forward.

Awkwardly holding her guitar case in front of her and her suitcase behind, Natty edged along the aisle. She wished she were really in the 1950s, when a gentleman would have risen from his seat to help her. But no; everyone either watched her progress with amusement or kept their eyes on their newspapers or the window. She'd been cursed with being born into an age without manners.

The doors clunked behind her as Natty made her way into the second and third carriage, where the crowd began to thin out. Eventually finding an empty booth, she flopped down gratefully beside the window.

For a moment, Natty closed her eyes, exhausted. Then she quickly straightened her posture, and whipped out a silver compact to check that neither her hair nor her make-up had been ruffled by her exertion. The day Natty Smalls put comfort before style would be a very bad day indeed!

And today was a good day — wasn't it? Her great escape!

Natty gazed out of the window at the passing back gardens of grimy terraced houses. The train was rolling along a tall embankment, and the slate-grey rooftops of London seemed to stretch endlessly beneath a similarly-coloured sky.

Natty liked trains. Her all-time favourite film was *Brief Encounter*, but there were so many others in which a train was the very embodiment of romance. The station scene in *Casablanca* was another that sprang to her mind whenever she was rushing along a busy platform.

As the inner-city Victorian terraces

gave way to the 1930s semis of suburbia, Natty imagined she was in a proper oldfashioned compartment, with a sliding door from the corridor, saggy chintzy seats and shiny walls turned from cream to brown by nicotine stains. She could almost hear the piercing steam whistle and throaty chug of a smoke-belching engine up front.

But the hard nylon seats and the rumble of the diesel engine vibrating through the floor made the fantasy hard to sustain. And as the suburbs gave way to fields and trees, and the exhilaration of her escape from London subsided, reality began to set in to Natty's thoughts, too.

With a heavy sigh, she gazed at the suitcase on the floor. A battered charity shop find, its cracked brown leather was mostly hidden beneath a wall-papering of colourful retro travel stickers — Rio de Janeiro, Paris, Los Angeles, New York, Rome.

The sad truth was, Natty had bought the stickers in an emporium of retro kitsch on the Kings Road in Chelsea. London was as far as she'd got — and now she was running away like a scalded cat.

★ ★ ★

Natty passed the journey to the coast with a vintage scene magazine, but for once even the glamour shots of retro clothes, rockabilly tattoos and mid-century American hot rods offered little escape from her increasingly downbeat mood. As the train began to trundle through familiar provincial suburbs, Natty's gloom deepened.

In the distance, amid a brown brick council estate, she glimpsed her old school and the little parade of local shops where she'd bought sweets as a kid. Even as a seven-year-old, Natty was obsessed with the old black-and-white films she found on satellite TV on wet afternoons when she'd bunk off school pretending to be ill. Her heroines were Rita Hayworth, Jean Harlow, Lauren

Bacall and Marilyn Monroe. At the age of eight, Natty's party piece was pouting and reciting Marilyn's lines from *How To Marry A Millionaire*.

It was a pity the film hadn't given much insight into the behaviour of real-life millionaires, Natty reflected sadly.

Craning her neck as the train rolled around a wide curve, Natty caught a fleeting sight of her parents' house. It brought back memories of the years she'd spent there watching trains like the one she was on now. How she'd longed, as a child, to be on one of the express trains leaving town for the bright lights of the capital! How disappointed the kid she'd been would be now, to see her older self coming home, defeated.

As the train slid into the faded splendour of a large Victorian station and came to a halt, Natty took her time getting her things together. There was no rush. It was the end of the line.

She put on a pair of 1950s Twinco

sunglasses. She'd bought them in Camden Market for the sparkly gold detailing on the pointed frames. Today, she was more grateful for the impenetrable, jet-black lenses. The day had grown sunny. But more importantly, she wanted something to hide behind.

But Natty wasn't one to be down for long. Melancholy wasn't a look that went with her clothes, and there was nothing like the hug of a tight girdle and the demands of stiletto heels for making a girl stand straight and hold her chin up high. As she left the train, heard the screeches of seagulls and filled her lungs with the briny air of the seaside, Natty felt a resurgence of optimism.

By the time she reached the sunny station steps, Natty had formulated a plan that, for the first time that day, looked further ahead than turning up unannounced on her mum's doorstep.

At the foot of the steps, Natty wistfully surveyed the queue of waiting taxis. In an ideal world she would click her fingers to alert one of the cabbies, command him to load her suitcase and guitar case in the back and tell him to take her to the Imperial Hotel on the seafront. Once there, she would instruct the doorman to collect her bags and pay the driver, then sweep regally into the towering Edwardian lobby to demand the penthouse suite for an indefinite period.

'Does Madam require anything else?' the rather handsome desk clerk would ask, solemnly, as he rose from his chair and bowed, his eyes lowered in deference.

'Only to be left alone with my broken heart,' she would reply in a sultry tone.

Unfortunately, in the real world, being dressed like a million dollars didn't equate to having anything like that amount in cash — Natty's credit card was maxed. She would have to spend at least the first couple of nights at her mum and dad's — and she'd have to get there on foot or by bus. But permanently regressing to the life of a teenager in her old bedroom wasn't an option for a smart and sophisticated twenty-one-year-old girl-about-town like her. Natty Smalls needed her independence.

From a man in a kiosk on the corner of a busy crossroads outside the station, Natty bought a local paper to commence her search for cool town-centre accommodation and a job to go with it. She could have looked for those things in London, but it was too scary. Starting afresh in her home town felt safer. She wanted to put as many miles as possible between herself and David Royale.

'Nice look!' said the cheery newspaper vendor, as Natty tucked the paper under her arm and bent to pick up her cases.

'Thanks!' Natty grinned, gratefully. The wonderful thing about making an effort with her clothes was that the compliments from total strangers always seemed to come at the exact moment when she really needed them.

'Going to a fancy dress party?' the vendor chortled.

Stung, Natty shot him a look over the top of her sunglasses.

'No,' she replied curtly, eyeing his drab, grey hoodie and sweat pants with disdain. 'Why? Are you going jogging?'

The vendor laughed and put his hands up in surrender. 'Just kidding, love! That Fifties look's really in at the moment — especially around here. Are you in a band?'

Natty relaxed and smiled. 'No, I just play for fun.'

'Have fun, then.'

'I'll try!' Natty trilled in her distinctive sing-song voice.

Skipping daintily across the road at the lights, Natty headed down the high street towards the sea, in search of somewhere to sit and go through the small ads.

Rather pleased with her speedy retort to the newspaper seller, Natty's mood brightened. She began looking forward to viewing some stylish urban pads.

Top floor would be nice, overlooking a winding cobbled lane in the chic part of town, with a French café on the ground floor that served really strong coffee, and a vintage shop or two further down the road. She'd have waxed floorboards and rugs, a rubber plant in a terracotta pot and an oak-veneered radiogram on which to play her collection of original LPs: Buddy Holly, Connie Francis and Patsy Cline.

That such a place would cost squilions she didn't have was a detail Natty would only confront when she was forced to. She knew the best her budget would stretch to would be a grotty room in a half-derelict house full of students.

As she walked, a little melody came into Natty's head that she thought might be the beginning of a song. Under her breath, she sang a line that sounded like a chorus. 'Everybody deserves a second chance . . . '

Thinking positively, Natty wondered

if that was what coming home was — a second chance. She certainly hoped so. Almost at the prom, she glimpsed between the passing open-topped tourist buses a place she didn't recall seeing before.

Matt's! read the sign in big, swirly red letters on a pink background. *Ice Cream, Shakes, Coffee & Cakes!* To the left of the sign was a cartoon rockabilly guy with a blond quiff, holding an outsize milkshake. To the right was a flirty-looking cartoon waitress with a raven-coloured ponytail, bearing a giant banana split on a tray. The window was framed in chrome and obscured by a picture of a scrumptious-looking strawberry sundae and the words *Indulge Yourself!*.

And why not! thought Natty. It looked like her sort of joint. She hadn't had so much as a coffee since breakfast, and lugging a trunk-size suitcase and guitar case was thirsty work. As she dodged the cars and taxis to cross the road, she realised she was starving.

Natty was about to go in when she

saw a sheet of A4 paper taped to the inside of the glass door.

Room To Rent
Suit artist, musician or similar.
Apply within.

That sounded good to Natty, and so did the music that greeted her as she put her shoulder to the door — Jerry Lee Lewis's 1957 smash *Whole Lotta Shakin' Goin' On.*

It was lunchtime and the ice-cream parlour was busy, mostly with young mums and toddlers. The floor space between the white Formica-topped tables was jammed with buggies and wooden high chairs. It looked like a crèche. But the decor was pure rock'n'roll, as if she'd stepped into a Hollywood musical version of a mid-twentieth-century American diner. Diamond-pattern pink and white tiles lined the walls, interspersed with big mirrors and glazed charcoal drawings of Elvis, Buddy Holly and Little Richard. Vinyl high stools in retro reds and blues stood at a chrome bar inside the window, while dotted around the walls were a vintage Wurlitzer jukebox and a gumball machine.

To Natty it was heaven. Swaying her hips to the piano-pumping music, she sashayed to the counter. She was just setting her cases on the floor when a loud 'Aaagh!' emanated from behind a display cabinet full of sticky goodies.

Natty jumped in surprise as the most handsome man she'd ever seen reeled into view. A rock'n'roll vision in black vintage jeans and a tight white T-shirt, he had snake-like hips, gym-built shoulders, a square jaw, chiselled cheek bones, vanilla-blond hair cut in a short back and sides with a rockabilly flat top . . . and a big white clown nose made of whipped cream.

'What's so funny?' he asked, looking slightly shell-shocked, as Natty burst out laughing.

'Um . . . do you know you've got a . . . ' she pointed to her nose.

He crossed his bright blue eyes and

rubbed his nose with the back of his wrist.

'Has it all gone?'

'Apart from the bit in your eyebrow.' Natty giggled. 'And the blob on your chin.'

She pulled a paper napkin from a chrome dispenser on the counter and handed it to him. He took it gratefully and wiped his face. He held up a canister.

'Just having a little battle with the whipped cream and it went off in my face. Story of my life, really. So . . . what can I get you?'

Natty perused the day's specials, chalked on a blackboard behind the counter.

'What's in Matt's Sundae Surprise?'

'Well, that would spoil the surprise, wouldn't it?' the ice-cream man shot back, with a grin. 'It's got a little bit of everything, actually. Strawberries, peaches, passion fruit, ice cream, chocolate, nuts.'

Natty's stomach rumbled. 'Mmmm, I'll have one of those!'

'Great! I like a girl who doesn't worry about her figure!'

Metaphorically slapped for the second time that day, Natty put her fists on her hips. 'I could take my custom elsewhere, you know?'

The man blushed like a tomato. 'Oops, that came out badly, didn't it? I meant to say a girl who doesn't *have* to worry about her figure! Because you've obviously got a great . . . not that I was looking at it or being personal . . . '

He tailed off with a look of abject embarrassment on his face and they both burst out laughing.

Natty put his verbal clumsiness down to nervousness, and she could forgive him that. He was such a gorgeous specimen she was feeling quite giddy herself. Fighting to contain the butterflies dancing in her stomach, Natty jerked her thumb over her shoulder.

'I also wondered . . . is the room still available?'

'It certainly is!' The ice-cream man grinned, eagerly. 'It's my mum's place, on St George's Street, just along the road from the station.'

He glanced at a metal-rimmed wall clock with a portrait of Marilyn Monroe printed on its face. 'She should be there at the moment. I'll give her a call if you like, and you can pop over after you've had your sundae.'

'That would be wonderful, thanks.'

'No problem. I'm Matt, by the way.'

'Interesting surname,' said Natty.

'Er-?' Matt looked blank.

'Bytheway,' explained Natty. 'Just a joke. I'm Natty.'

'Very natty from where I'm standing!' Matt agreed with a grin. He gazed at her fur-trimmed leopard-print coat and pencil dress a moment longer than strictly necessary, as if he wasn't so much admiring her clothes as mesmerised by the hour-glass figure inside them.

'Natty Smalls,' added Natty.

'I can imagine,' Matt sighed, wistfully. Snapping out of his trance, he blushed and said, 'Take a seat! I'll bring your sundae over when it's ready.'

There was an old-fashioned wooden hat and coat stand just inside the door. Natty stowed her suitcase and guitar case beside it and hung up her coat. She wasn't sure if the day was warming up or whether it was just her, but the sudden liveliness of her circulation was giving her a very nice feeling.

The yummy mummies and toddlers had mainly occupied the tables, and there was a stool free at the bar inside the window. Welcoming the chance to pose in an elevated position, Natty slid elegantly onto the vinyl and crossed her smoke-coloured nylon-stockinged thighs, the better to show off a shapely calf defined by a pinstripe seam.

She tried to look cool and serene, but found she couldn't take her eyes off Matt as he prepared her sundae. He had his back to her and above a tall display cabinet Natty could only see the closely cropped back of his head, but even that was more gorgeous than most people's faces.

Mentally, Natty began ticking boxes.

Tall, blond and handsome — tick. Rockabilly haircut and vintage jeans — tick. Not only does he work in a super-cool American-style ice-cream parlour, but judging from his name he appears to own it!

It wasn't that Natty was only attracted to wealthy men, of course — she'd never consider herself shallow. But a childhood diet of Hollywood romances had taught her there were certain minimum standards of lifestyle that a girl should aspire to!

It was true that Matt seemed a bit shy and nervous, and was maybe on the clumsy side, but his goofiness struck her as cute and reassuringly unthreatening. In her fantasies Natty was always being swept off her feet by dark-haired, confident, clever and ruthless types like Bogart or the Bond-era Sean Connery. To her recent cost, however, she'd found that real-life ruthless types like David Royale could be a bit too confident, clever and ruthless for comfort.

As Matt came around the counter,

carrying a tray and a towering concoction in a tall glass, Natty took the opportunity to drink in the sight of his tall, gym-sculpted body from his brushed-up blond flat top to a pair of black, suede-topped crepe-soled shoes.

'That looks delicious!' Natty enthused. She hoped he took her to mean the sundae as she mentally applied a pen to another box on her checklist. Chemistry to make a girl combust — tick, tick and tick!

'I phoned Mum and you can go and have a look at the room as soon as you're ready,' Matt ventured, as he put the sundae on the bar.

'Great!' Desperate to prolong the conversation before he disappeared back behind the counter, Natty blurted, 'So . . . this is your ice-cream parlour, is it?'

'Unless somebody changed the name on the sign after I came in!' Matt grinned.

He was standing very close to her, his jeans so close to her stockinged knee that he was almost creating a static charge in the nylon. Natty felt herself heating up like a furnace with a glow that spread from her stomach to her cheeks.

But before Natty could speak, a bell jangled and the door burst open. In rushed a tall, slim, angry woman with raven-black hair tied back in a sleek ponytail. In her arms was a screaming, wet-faced girl of about four, whom she thrust into Matt's arms with enough force to rock him on his heels.

'I'm sorry, Matt, you'll have to look after her — I just can't do anything with her today!'

'Jen!' Matt protested, as he clutched the child. But the woman turned and left the parlour as quickly as she came in.

Reeling in shock, Natty watched the woman's red cheeks and black ponytail fly past the window like a tornado. When Natty turned back, Matt was bouncing and kissing the little girl, whose tantrum seemed to be subsiding.

'Oh well, Rosie,' crooned Matt, 'it

looks like you're stuck with Daddy for the afternoon.'

Raising his eyebrows to Natty in apology for the unexpected interruption, Matt carried his daughter towards the counter. As he turned, every ray of light in the ice-cream parlour seemed to converge on a plain gold ring on the third finger of his left hand.

Watching his retreating back, even the boa-constrictor grip of her girdle couldn't stop Natty slumping as all her hopes rushed from her like air from a balloon.

The final box on her mental checklist yawned emptily. Single — um, no.

There was no way she was leaving that box un-ticked again. With a sigh, she turned to the consolation prize of her ice-cream sundae. At least this time she'd found out before she made a complete fool of herself.

2

St George's was a busy road that crossed the top of the high street. The address Matt gave Natty was just a few doors down from the crossroads where she'd bought her paper earlier. It was a tall mid-terraced Victorian house that must once have been grand, and was still imposing. It had steps up to a large red front door, three rows of sash windows, railings around some basement windows, and dormer windows in the grey slate roof. The proportions were as perfect as a doll's house, and Natty's spirits lifted at the sight of it.

With the taxis and tourist buses queuing outside waiting for the traffic lights to change, and pedestrians hurrying along the pavement to and from the station, it was just the sort of chic town centre residence Natty had always dreamed of living in.

With her suitcase in one hand and guitar case in the other, Natty trotted up the steps. She didn't have to put either of her burdens down to ring the doorbell because the door was snatched open from the inside as she approached.

A deafening blast of Abba's *Waterloo* hit Natty like a train. Matt's mum stood framed in the doorway — and Natty loved her on sight.

Standing a step above Natty, with her height boosted by white killer heels and her chin lifted with theatrical elegance, the woman looked ten times larger than life. She was in her fifties, Natty guessed, with blonde hair worn in a huge bouffant, an orange tan and a white dress that clung to every one of her many generous curves.

'I'm Margie!' the woman hollered over the music. 'You must be Natty! Matt's told me all about you! Come in, come in!'

Margie waved her cigarette around theatrically. 'You don't mind smoking, do you? It's a filthy habit, but I can't give it up!'

'It doesn't bother me,' said Natty. She'd tried smoking once, at school, nearly choked to death, felt sick for days and sworn never to touch the weed again. But all Natty's heroines in those old black and white films had smoked, and in the right hands an elegantly-held cigarette and a perfectly-blown smoke ring still struck her as the height of sophistication.

Natty could barely smell the smoke through the cloud of perfume that greeted her as she crossed the threshold. Margie had disappeared down the hallway.

'Chuck your bags anywhere!' Margie called, as Abba was abruptly turned down. 'There, we can talk now!'

Natty followed Margie's voice into a living room painted entirely white — walls, floorboards, bookshelves, piano — as if someone had taken a six-inch brush to the lot in a single spontaneous session.

'Wow!' said Natty, turning to take in the arctic glare.

The room had a big bay window

overlooking the street, and was dominated by a canvas on an artist's easel. On the floor around the easel was scattered an untidy assortment of paint tubes, brushes, cups and empty wine glasses. The overpowering scent of linseed oil took Natty back to her old art room at school.

'Jude's our resident artist,' Margie announced. 'She lives in the basement but she works up here because the light's better.'

The back of the easel was facing into the room and Natty skipped over to the window to see what was on the other side of the canvas.

'I used to love painting at school,' Natty enthused. 'I used to paint all these long thin femme-fatales with furs and elegant cigarette holders.'

'Jude's more into naked men,' explained Margie.

'So I see!' Natty regarded the half finished painting with raised eyebrows.

'Jude teaches a life class,' Margie explained.

'Do you have many people living here?' Natty asked.

'Well, there's Jude, our artist. Then there's Jase, who has the attic. Jase is a DJ. He has a gig at that new club, Space. That's why I put the bit about artists and musicians on the ad. I've got this vision of a house full of creative people, sharing ideas, discussing art, sitting up all night playing music!'

'Sounds wonderful!' Natty agreed.

'And you're a musician!' Margie enthused. 'We can have jam sessions!'

'Maybe!' Natty trilled, and wished she hadn't walked in carrying a guitar case. Natty liked being the centre of attention — for her clothes. Her singing and song-writing were things that had never left the privacy of her bedroom. The prospect of sharing it with a houseful of strangers was terrifying.

'Oh,' Margie added as an after-thought, 'Matt's staying here at the moment, too.'

'Matt lives here?' Natty blurted.

Margie beckoned urgently with her

cigarette. 'Let me show you the rest of the house!'

Momentarily stunned by the thought of sharing a house with the most gorgeous man she'd ever met — albeit a married one — she gathered herself and hurried after the glamorous landlady.

The kitchen could have been a picture clipped from a 1950s magazine like *Practical Homemaker*. The room was big and spacious, the wooden cupboards were painted turquoise and topped with scrubbed oak worktops. The gas cooker was an enamel antique and there was a big, curvy American-style fridge.

'The kitchen of my dreams!' Natty exclaimed.

'I guess you'd call it retro.' Margie preened. 'A few years ago it was just old!'

Margie smiled fondly at a framed picture on the breakfast bar of a man with a bald head and thick beard. 'My late husband, Alf.' She introduced him as warmly and casually as if he were sitting there drinking coffee and reading a newspaper. 'He was much older than me, of course. He was the biscuit king of England at one point and I was the girl in the Coconut Crunch ads. You're too young to remember them.'

Natty looked closely at the landlady — and her face seemed to shimmer and rejuvenate before Natty's eyes. Suddenly, Natty was four years old, kneeling on her mum and dad's front-room carpet, gazing up at the television where a saucy-looking and impossibly glamorous blonde was nibbling a biscuit, saucer-size eyes gleaming as if it were the naughtiest thing in the world.

'That was you?' Natty asked in awe.

Margie struck a pose, imaginary biscuit raised to her mouth, hand cupped beneath her chin as she recited the slogan in a husky tone, 'Don't let the crumbs give you away!'

Natty clapped her hands and squealed. 'I've never met anyone famous before!'

'Well, there were three of us, actually. You probably remember one of the later ones.' Margie waved her cigarette dismissively. 'Oh, it was a long time ago. In the end, all we had left were the crumbs. And now poor Alf's gone, too.'

Margie looked on the point of tears. Natty felt a stab of pain on her behalf. She was about to give the landlady a comforting hug when Margie took a long drag on her cigarette and pulled herself together.

'But we can't look back, can we? And you know what? I'm loving life at the moment. I spent a year rattling around this place on my own. Then I decided to fill the house with life and people. That's when I took all my widow's weeds to the charity shop and decided that from now on I'd only ever wear white!'

'It must be comforting for you having Matt and his wife here,' said Natty.

'His wife?' Margie's face creased in maternal concern. 'Unfortunately Matt and Jen are going through a bit of a difficult time . . . so he's staying here on his own while they try to sort things out.'

'Matt's separated?' Natty blurted.

'I shouldn't be telling you,' said Margie anxiously. 'I just hope they can work things out for Rosie's sake — that's my granddaughter. She's such a beautiful child.'

'I know. I met her at the ice-cream parlour.' Natty had never considered herself the most maternal of women — sticky toddlers and vintage fashion didn't mix. But after her initial shock at Jen's arrival in the parlour, she'd found herself utterly entranced by Matt's daughter.

'Matt's a great dad, isn't he?' Natty sighed, wistfully.

'Oh, he's a wonderful boy,' Margie said proudly. 'It's such a shame, the way things have gone for him and Jen. I always thought he was making a mistake. But I try not to interfere in my son's life. Have you ever been married, Natty?'

'Nearly!' With a crashing sigh, she admitted, 'Unfortunately it turned out he wasn't as single as he said he was.'

'Ah.' Margie's face was a picture of

sympathy. 'And that's why you're looking for a room? I'd better show it to you, then.'

Twirling in a swirl of smoke and perfume, Margie led the way to the first floor.

'You're right under Matt!' said Margie, as she pushed open a door at the front of the house. 'This was Cheryl's room — my youngest. She went to uni in London and decided to stay there.'

'Lucky thing,' said Natty, thinking of her own ill-fated time in the capital. 'But lucky me!'

Flooded with sun from a huge sash window overlooking the street, the room was painted in pinks and mauves with a big bed covered by the fattest duvet Natty had ever seen. There was a massive antique wardrobe and, most important of all, a generous Queen Anne dressing table with a big gilt-edged oval mirror. There was even a vanity wash basin — everything a makeup obsessed girl could want.

'I'll take it!' Natty exclaimed. Shyly,

34

she added, 'If you'll have me, that is.'

Margie looked momentarily concerned. 'I'm supposed to take references . . . '

She waved her doubts away with her cigarette. 'What the heck! Matt likes you, I like you — bring up your cases! I'm cooking dinner for everyone tonight, so you can meet the others then.'

★   ★   ★

As Natty unpacked her case and filled the big wardrobe with fifty-year-old fabrics, she sang excitedly the little chorus that had been going around her head all day, 'Everybody deserves a second chance!'

'Well Natty Smalls,' she said to her reflection in the dressing table mirror, 'it looks as if your prayers have been answered — some of them, anyway!'

Having expected to wind up in a grotty hovel, her room looked like the Ritz. First thing tomorrow, she'd go round to her mum's and pick up all the clothes she hadn't been able to take to

London. She had a ton of them.

In the meantime Natty deliberated over what to wear for her first dinner with Margie . . . and, more importantly, with Matt. Matt who may or may not be as married and off-limits as she'd initially thought.

She opted to step a decade further back in time with a calf-length black wool dress from the Second World War that she'd picked up in London. Fastened at the front with big mother-of-pearl buttons, it had a wide circular collar defined with white piping and slightly puffed short sleeves, simultaneously demure yet cut to enhance the idealised hour-glass figure of the era. Teamed with dotted black stockings and highly shone court shoes, it was a real forces' sweetheart look, Natty thought.

Her hair could stay the same — the rolled and curled style spanned the Forties and Fifties, but she swapped the orchid for a big bow in navy silk with white polka dots. She scrubbed off her day make-up and replaced it with smoky and sophisticated evening shades.

Practising a seductive, sleepy-eyed look, Natty pouted at herself in the mirror and hoped Matt had a thing for Rita Hayworth. He looked like the kind of guy who might.

As Natty descended the stairs, she was met by a delicious aroma of curry and the sound of Abba turned up full blast. From the kitchen, Margie's powerful rock soprano soared above the vocals of the group.

Emerging from the steam in flip flops and chef's whites, Margie looked at Natty's dress with open admiration.

'Natty, you are setting the bar far too high for the rest of us!'

'I try my best!'

'Is that a Christian Dior girdle?' asked Margie, regarding Natty with an expert eye.

Natty was taken aback.

'I haven't told you about my shop, have I?' Margie explained. 'Posh Knickers, in Lower Goat Lane. I do all the stockings and petticoats for the rock'n'roll crowd. You'll have to pop in. Now go and meet Jude and Jase while I get changed for dinner.'

Jude may live in the basement and Jase in the attic, but they were obviously very close, Natty decided. In the cosy gloom of a candle-lit dining room, Jude's long, languid frame was draped across a big squishy sofa, with a sketch pad propped on her belly and her bare feet dumped in the lap of the balding Jase, who was reading a newspaper.

They were both in their early forties, Natty guessed. Jase was casually dressed in plain black T-shirt, black jeans and rigger boots. Jude had on a long, thin and faded hippy-like print dress. Her hair was the biggest explosion of chocolate brown curls Natty had ever seen. It framed a narrow face tanned the colour of teak.

'Sorry I can't get up,' said Jase, as he offered his hand with a friendly smile. 'I'm posing.'

Jude turned her sketch pad around with a toothy grin. 'What do you think?'

Natty went to Jude's end of the sofa to look at Jase's profile from her angle.

'Has she captured my noble manliness?' Jase asked, wiggling his head camply.

'Consider yourself captured!' Natty confirmed.

Jase waved a wine glass towards a dining table laden with bottles and glasses.

'Pour yourself a drink.' He indicated a vacant sofa opposite. 'Sit down, tell us all about yourself!'

'Thanks!' Natty poured herself a small glass of white and hoped it would calm her nerves. She'd hoped Matt would be waiting when she came downstairs and had geared herself up to making a good impression. She was disappointed he wasn't around, and felt a little jittery, expecting him to come into the room at any moment. She tried to put him out of her mind and told herself it was just as important to get to know her other new housemates.

Gingerly, Natty perched on the edge

of the vacant sofa. Wartime fashions weren't designed for squishy modern sofas and she hoped it wouldn't swallow her up. A lapful of white wine and stockinged legs pointing skyward would not be a good look!

'Margie tells me you're a musician,' said Jude, 'and that you're going to give us all a song later.'

'She did?' Natty squeaked. 'Well, it's not something I really do in public.'

'What kind of music are you into?' asked Jase.

'Oh, both kinds,' Natty joked. 'Rock . . . and roll!'

'Fifties, eh?' Jase said encouragingly.

'Jase is into all that modern disco trance stuff,' Jude explained, wrinkling her nose.

'You'll get on well with Matt!' Jase grinned.

'Matt's our very own Elvis about the house!' said Jude. 'Have you met him yet, Natty? Mmmmm. He's scrumptious!'

The rapturous expression on Jude's

deeply tanned face sent such a stab of jealousy through Natty that she wasn't sure how to respond.

'Jude wants Matt for her toy boy!' Jase joked.

Jude took a playful swipe at Jase with her sketch pad. 'Not so much of the toy boy — I'm not that old!'

'Is Matt single, then?' Natty fished for information.

'Why, are you looking for a boy-friend?' Jase asked, his expression full of interest.

'No!' Natty squealed. 'I just, um . . . well, I met his daughter at the ice-cream parlour.'

'It's a shame about Rosie,' Jude nodded. 'But he'd be crazy to go back to Jen. He could do so much better.'

'Like a nice older woman . . . ?' Jase tickled Jude's feet.

'In my dreams!' Jude admitted with a sigh. She plumped up her frizz of chocolate curls. 'Unfortunately there's no shortage of competition.'

Jude gave Natty a level look, and

added, 'Matt's the most wanted man in town.'

'Really?' Natty wondered if the comment was meant as a warning, and whether Jude was serious competition.

Although Jude was much older than Matt, there was a seductive confidence in the way she was draped barefoot across the sofa. Her tanned face had a sun-lover's lines around her eyes but, with not a spare ounce of flesh on her, her face had a striking bone structure. In the soft candlelight, Jude was an undeniably attractive woman.

Margie sailed into the room wearing an extravagant white evening dress and a pair of cat-shaped oven mitts in which she was holding a steaming casserole dish full of curry.

'Grab the plates and cutlery, will you, Jase?'

'Your wish is my command, mistress,' said Jase, untangling himself from Jude's legs.

'Can I carry anything?' Natty offered, springing to her feet.

'No, no, you're a guest,' scolded Margie. 'Just sit yourself down and have some more wine.'

When the table was laden and they'd all taken their seats, Margie said, 'We don't always do this, Natty, but I think it's nice to eat together whenever we can — it makes it like a family. Sometimes Jase or Jude cook, or we get a takeaway. The rest of the time, treat the kitchen as your own. Tea, coffee and milk are in with the rent as long as they're there.'

'Anything else, write your name on it,' said Jase.

'You make it sound like my Cheryl's house when she was at uni,' Margie chuckled. 'One egg in the fridge with someone else's name written on it in felt pen! Did you go to uni, Natty?'

'Only the university of life!' Natty chirped.

'University of hard knocks in my case!' Jase joked.

'Borstal in mine,' Jude chimed in. 'Looks like we're all underachievers together.'

Margie gazed around the table and sighed. 'It's such a shame Matt's not here to welcome you to the house, Natty, but he's gone to dinner with Jen.'

'Has he? Oh, well, never mind.' Natty tried to sound unconcerned. She'd just got used to the idea that Matt was separated and available.

Jude swished her frizz of chocolate curls over her narrow shoulders and said, casually, 'Are they getting back together again, then?'

Natty watched Margie closely, holding her breath while she waited for the answer.

'I think it's some kind of make or break meeting,' Margie confirmed. 'I just hope they can sort things out.'

Or not, thought Natty, crossing her fingers beneath the dining room table.

It wasn't that she didn't want Matt to be happy. Picturing his chiselled, grinning face, vanilla blond rockabilly flat top and shy, goofy blushes, Natty wanted him to be the happiest man in the world. She'd just prefer him to be happy with *her*.

In Natty's book, relationships that needed 'working at' seldom worked in the long run — you were just prolonging the agony. You were better off making a clean break and starting afresh, as she'd done as soon as she'd found out the truth about David Royale.

Natty decided not to air her opinion in front of Matt's mum, though. She didn't want to give away her feelings, and as the new girl in the house she didn't want to rock the boat, either.

'But let's not worry about Matt,' Margie said brightly. 'We haven't toasted our new housemate yet.'

'To Natty!' Jase declared, as they clinked their four glasses together across the table.

'And to all of us!' Margie added.

'All for one and one for all!' cheered Jase.

'Four singletons together!' added Jude, enthusiastically.

'But hopefully not single for long!' Natty replied.

'Oooh,' Jase cooed. 'Is there someone special?'

Natty fluttered her false eyelashes and said, coyly, 'Just saying we should all keep our hopes up!'

'I'll second that,' said Jude, 'although it's a lot easier to feel that way at your age, Natty, than it is when you get to mine!'

Natty glanced from Jude to Jase. 'Are you two not . . . ?'

Jude and Jase exploded with laughter.

'You must be joking!' they exclaimed as one.

'I'd have to kill him!'

'*Her!*'

'No.' Jude sighed. 'I'm afraid Jase and I are just a couple of sad old cast-off divorcees that no one else wants.'

'Washed up like beached starfish on the rock of Margie's hospitality,' Jase agreed.

'Oh, don't be like that, you two!' Margie said briskly. With a wink at Natty, she added, 'I'm sure someone will want the pair of you — eventually!'

For the next hour, Natty tried to banish her mental image of Matt and his wife having a romantic reunion meal, and concentrated on getting to know her new housemates.

She quickly found she liked all of them. Whether Jude had serious designs on Matt or not, Natty couldn't tell, but the fact that she never knew when Jude was being serious was part of her charm. Jude said such outrageous things in such a laid-back manner that Natty couldn't help warming to her.

Jase was sweet, quipping and joking his way through dinner and getting redder, sillier and drunker as the evening went on. It turned out he wasn't a famous DJ, or even a full-time one. He worked in a menswear shop. Spinning discs in a club once a week was something he did on the side.

'You've got to start somewhere, though, haven't you?' Jase slurred, as he swirled red wine around in his glass. 'I just wish I'd done it twenty years ago, when I was your age, Natty.'

'What did you do instead?' Natty asked.

'Got married, got a mortgage, got a high-stress job and spent the next twenty years living the life everybody else thought I was supposed to be living,' he replied with a shrug of his shoulders.

'We'd all like to go back to Natty's age and do things differently,' declared Jude. 'I know I wouldn't have married Colin, although I was pregnant with Carla by then so I didn't really have a choice.'

Natty smiled sympathetically, and not for the first time wondered if she'd had a lucky escape from David. Even if he hadn't been leading a double life, would she really have been happy living with him in ten or twenty years' time? Meeting people of Jude's and Jase's age whose lives were full of regret made the prospect of making any kind of commitment scary.

Margie cut through the suddenly sombre mood of the dinner with a brisk, 'Don't listen to these old moaners, Natty. I don't regret anything I've ever done — and neither will you, if you follow your heart.'

Natty grinned gratefully. She was certainly glad she'd followed her heart in coming back to her home town.

'Now, who's for dessert?' Margie asked.

While Margie bustled off to the kitchen, Natty decided her new landlady was the perfect hostess. Throughout the meal she'd been saucy, flirtatious, entertaining and interested in everything everybody said, while all the while exuding a glamorous theatricality that Natty admired.

Natty would never say a bad word about her own family — they'd always done their best for her. But she couldn't help wishing she had a mother as flamboyant as Margie. She wondered if having her as a mother-in-law was too much to hope for, because she'd surely never find a better one. There was such a warmth around Margie's dinner table that she was already beginning to feel like part of the family.

Natty was helping the others carry the used dishes into the kitchen when the front door opened with a clatter and closed with a loud slam. Jumping at the noise, she turned to see Matt standing at the end of the long, tiled hall.

Her stomach flipped at the sight of him. His broad shoulders and muscular chest were emphasised by a zip-adorned black leather biker jacket hanging open over a tight white T-shirt. His narrow hips and long athletic legs were enhanced by black drainpipe jeans.

But there was something different about him that made Natty's heart begin to thump. The chiselled but happy-go-lucky face she remembered from the ice-cream parlour was pained and downcast.

Noticing her, Matt looked embarrassed and suddenly uncertain, like a rabbit caught in headlights. With a heavy sigh, he shrugged off his jacket and hung it on the post at the end of the stairs. He looked at Natty as if he really wanted to head up to his room. Instead, he seemed to gather himself and came down the hall towards the kitchen.

'Hi, Natty. You liked the room, then?' He gave her a friendly grin, but it was a pale ghost of the grin that he'd worn so readily earlier that day. Natty felt every bit of the pain he was so clearly trying to conceal.

'It's perfect,' she breathed, her heart in her throat.

She wished she could hug him and soothe away what had clearly been a bruising evening for him, but she didn't dare. She hardly knew him, after all.

'Wan' a beer, mate?' slurred Jase, yanking open the big American fridge.

'Cor, yeah!' Matt took the proffered bottle, levered off the cap and took a grateful gulp.

'How did it go?' asked Margie, although to Natty the answer was plainly written on Matt's face.

'As expected.' Matt sighed again.

'Awww, Matt!' Margie wrapped her

51

arms around her son and propped her chin on his muscled chest. 'Come and sit down and talk about it.'

Embarrassed, Matt disentangled himself. 'No, don't let me spoil the party. I'll just go upstairs and unwind a bit.'

'You're sure you're all right?' Margie pleaded.

'Yes, of course I am!' Matt gave his mother a reassuring grin and Natty was relieved to see that his smile looked more natural this time. Whatever the emotional beating he'd taken this evening, he really was an easy-going, light-hearted guy.

'Well, I'm glad you're settling in, Natty,' he said, turning back to her. 'That's a great dress, by the way.'

'Thanks!'

'Puts the rest of us to shame, doesn't she?' Margie added warmly, looking at Natty.

Natty barely heard the landlady, because at that moment her eyes had met Matt's. He looked raw and shaken, but the look in his eyes was one Natty had never seen before, from anyone. Every other sight and sound seemed to fade out and for a long moment she thought time in the kitchen had stopped. Her breathing definitely had.

Eventually, Matt said, 'Well, I'll catch up with you tomorrow, Natty. See the rest of you guys in the morning.'

★   ★   ★

Upstairs later on, Natty sat at her dressing table in her bullet bra and high-waisted 1950s-style knickers carefully removing her foundation and primer and moisturising her skin. She always enjoyed the hour or so that she spent putting on and taking off her face at the beginning and end of each day. It was a calming, meditative oasis of me-time, a throwback to a more glamorous and feminine age that had largely been forgotten by today's over-rushed, multi-tasking women. They didn't know what they were missing, Natty thought.

She hummed a cheery melody as she

leaned towards the mirror over her collection of pots, tubs, bottles, tweezers, blotting papers, pencils and brushes of every size.

She had more brushes than Michaelangelo, but then she saw her face as a canvas and her make-up as an artistic endeavour. Well, you couldn't create a masterpiece without the right tools.

Natty enjoyed lounging in her retro lingerie, too. The fabrics, cut and colours — pale lemon with a delicate pattern of tea roses today — were too beautiful to be covered up all day, even if the only audience was her. Her bullet bra was nothing short of an architectural design classic! Flaunting it in the privacy of her bedroom made her feel as glamorous as Betty Page, the legendary cheesecake pin-up upon whom the cartoon character Betty Boop was based. She felt particularly upbeat this evening, knowing that Matt, the most gorgeous man in the world, was just feet away in the bedroom above hers.

She felt sorry for him. Natty knew

what it was like to invest everything you had in a relationship and have it thrown back in your face. She knew it must be even worse with a child involved.

But it did mean that Matt was a lot more single than she'd thought! And the good news for him was . . . so was she!

'Well Natty Smalls,' Natty told her reflection, 'it looks as if this could be your second chance after all!'

The face that grinned back at her from the mirror was one the rest of the world hadn't seen since her school days — a fresh-faced girl with normal-sized eyelashes, no eyeshadow, un-rouged lips and nude cheeks lightly dusted with freckles instead of peachy foundation and coral blusher.

The girl in the glass looked as innocent as a fifteen-year-old and Natty was suddenly struck by the sensation of moving back in time, as if all the pain and disappointment of London and David Royale had been washed away with her mascara.

Without warning, some more words floated into Natty's mind to fit that little melody she'd been humming since she arrived at the coast. While they were fresh in her mind, she sprang from the chair and heaved her guitar case onto the bed.

Nestling in purple velvet, her replica Fifties Gretsch was a thing of beauty, a hollow-bodied electric guitar finished in sunburst orange beneath a lacquer as deep and polished as a mirror. With its twin sound holes in the shape of music clefts, and fittings finished in chrome, it was a true rock'n'roll instrument as played by all the greats from Chuck Berry and Eddie Cochran in the Fifties to rockabilly revivalist Brian Setzer of the Stray Cats.

Natty lifted the heavy instrument carefully. It was the most expensive thing she'd ever owned. She felt a little twinge of guilt for keeping it. Perhaps she should have left it in David's flat with the so-called engagement ring. But a present was a present and she'd taken nothing else from him.

Sitting on the bed near the head-board, Natty propped herself against the pillows and cradled the guitar in her lap. It was late, and she was conscious that Matt was in the room above hers, probably trying to sleep, but without plugging into an amplifier the steel strings wouldn't make too much noise if she strummed them softly.

Gingerly, she began playing a little four-chord riff, two downward strums on each chord. CC, GG, CC, FF.

The ring of the strings immediately excited her. As the repeated pattern settled into a catchy rhythm, it sounded like the beginning of a Buddy Holly song — always her benchmark for pop music perfection. At the same time, it was her own, too.

Softly, Natty began to sing in a light, clear soprano.

'I've been talking to the man upstairs.'
CC, GG, CC, FF.
'Telling him about all my worry and cares.'

CC, GG, CC, FF.
'*About my poor old broken heart,*
'*Don't you think I deserve* — '
She paused and dramatically slapped her palm across the strings to silence them and to tap on the wooden body at the same time.
' *— a second chance!*'
Vamping her little riff more confidently Natty wondered where she could take the song from there. Smiling mischievously, she pictured Matt, with his square jaw, white T-shirt and bulging biceps. On impulse, she struck a ringing and dramatic A chord to take the song in a bold new direction. *A bridge!* she thought. *Yes, that'll work.*
Gazing up at the ceiling, daring to send Matt a little message, if only in her mind, Natty started to sing again.
'*Then I saw you and my heart began to dance,*
'*Could this really be my second chance?*'
Giggling to herself, Natty reverted to her four-chord melody, strumming the

chords more enthusiastically now. A chorus came together of its own accord, the same line chanted over and over.

'Everybody deserves a second chance . . . yeah, yeah, yeah . . . everybody deserves a second chance . . . '

Realising she'd begun to sing and play a little loudly for the hour, Natty stilled the strings with her palm. Leaning back on her pillows, she closed her eyes and hugged the hard curvy body of the guitar to her belly. She'd need another verse to complete the song. But she was satisfied for now.

Silently, Natty kept time with her foot as the music continued to play in her head.

Could this really be my second chance . . . yeah, yeah, yeah!

Gazing longingly at the ceiling, she whispered, 'Could this really be *our* second chance?'

3

The next morning, the road outside Natty's window was jumping with traffic and the house was vibrating with the thrum of a vacuum cleaner.

Natty sprang out of bed in a sheer black baby-doll nightdress trimmed with fur. Retro glamour was a twenty-four-hour obsession for her. After all, she reasoned, supposing there was a fire and she had to evacuate during the night, she'd still want to feel like the star of a 1950s Hollywood movie, wouldn't she?

Natty slipped on a short silk kimono with a green and gold oriental pattern and opened her door a crack. She peered through to check the coast was clear for a sprint to the bathroom. It wasn't that she didn't want anyone — and particularly Matt — to see her barely dressed. It was that she didn't want anyone to see her with no make-up and her hair in a net!

In Natty's book, a woman owed it to herself to present an image of effortlessly achieved glamour at all times. A glimpse of the hard work behind the scenes would be like going to a red carpet night at a West End theatre and seeing Elizabeth Taylor walking across the foyer in a face pack, tatty dressing gown and carpet slippers. It would destroy the illusion.

Natty dreamed of a white wedding and a happy-ever-after in an enormous mansion, but she didn't want the big house as a status symbol. Although she longed for love and togetherness as much as the next girl, Natty couldn't see how any couple could keep the marital flame alive without separate bedrooms and bathrooms to preserve some mystery.

Horror to Natty was the thought of a make-up-free woman and a stubble-faced man sitting across a breakfast table in crumpled dressing gowns and bed hair. It was no wonder so many people got divorced!

Idly, Natty wondered how Matt would take to the idea of separate rooms. David Royale hadn't been keen. Then again, David hadn't been too enamoured of Natty's other belief — which was that a girl should save the ultimate mystery until her wedding night.

As he'd observed in his posh and sardonic tones, 'Virginity is a rather old-fashioned ideal.'

And as Natty had trilled across the dinner table in reply, 'I guess I'm just an old-fashioned girl!'

Given the way things had ended with David, Natty was glad she'd stuck to her principles.

With no one on the landing, Natty risked a glance over the banister. Margie was half way up the stairs, enthusiastically jabbing at the carpet with her vacuum cleaner nozzle and singing Gloria Gaynor's *I Will Survive* to the accompaniment of a radio turned up louder than the machine.

Margie was power-dressed in a white *Dynasty*-style jacket, matching above-the-knee skirt and high heels, her yellow-blonde hair a beach-ball-sized bouffant. Mingling with the burnt dust smell of the cleaner was a cloud of tangy perfume.

Now there was a woman after her own heart.

''Scuse me, Mum! Forgot something!' The top of Matt's blond flat top came bopping urgently up the stairs. As he danced around Margie, Natty leapt back from the banister and dived for the bathroom.

Matt reached the landing in time to catch a flash of green kimono and the pink soles of Natty's feet before she slammed the door.

Leaning back on the door, Natty let out a sigh of relief. Sharing a house with Matt was going to keep her on her toes!

A knuckle rapped on the door and she jumped with a yelp.

'Sorry Natty,' Matt called through

the door. 'You couldn't pass my car keys, could you? I think I left them on the back of the sink.'

'Just one moment!' Natty sang back.

Hiding behind the door, Natty opened it a few inches and snaked her wrist around the edge, Matt's key-ring looped over her little finger. *At least my fingernails are made up,* she thought with satisfaction.

'You're a star!' said Matt. As his fingers briefly touched hers Natty realised that sharing a house while preserving a little mystery was actually quite fun!

★ ★ ★

Natty always dressed up, but she didn't always dress girly. Back in her room, she squeezed herself into a pair of snug-hipped dark blue vintage jeans with a bold gold stitch, five-inch turn-ups and a three-inch black leather belt that sat high on her waist where a belt should sit.

Natty never wore a waistband lower than her belly button. Apart from the fact that anything lower wouldn't cover her giant retro knickers, it created totally the wrong shape in her opinion. She teamed the jeans with a short-sleeve pink gingham shirt, knotted under her bullet bust, and, having checked that her scarlet toenail gloss had suffered no dings, a pair of strappy gold high-heeled sandals.

Her orange orchid, perched in a glass of water overnight, was still fresh, so she dried the stem and pinned it in her ruby-red hair. Leaning in to her dressing table mirror to pencil in her beauty spot, she arched her freshly drawn eyebrows and formed her coral pink lips into a seductive kiss.

With shiny pastel blue eye shadow on her lids and salmon pink in the sockets, it was a real rockabilly girl look, all the better to knock the blue suede shoes off a rockabilly guy like Matt.

Natty had a quick fantasy about strutting into the kitchen like Olivia

Newton John in *Grease*, snapping her fingers and singing *You're The One That I Want* while Matt sat at the breakfast bar as entranced as John Travolta.

After an hour in the bath, though, and another hour putting on her face, Natty sauntered downstairs to find that Matt had long left for work — as had everyone else, it seemed. She wasn't too put out — she'd casually drop into the ice-cream parlour later.

In the meantime, Natty was happy to have the house to herself. As she strolled along the tiled hall, she felt like a proper lady of leisure. Not that she'd be one for long. If she wanted to pay the rent, she'd have to get a job and start tearing out of the door before nine, like everyone else.

Natty quite fancied herself as a radio reporter. She had a pinched-waist oatmeal pencil dress that would be perfect. Perhaps she could team it with black horn-rimmed specs and matching stilettos and put her hair in a bun for a late Fifties New York office look. She pictured herself running past American fire engines and police cars with a big furry microphone in her hand, chasing down the big story.

From radio it would be just a small leap to television. 'We're going now to ace reporter Natty Smalls, who is live from outside the White House . . . '

She didn't have any experience of reporting, but Natty didn't see that as a problem. She was certain that if you paid enough attention to looking great, doors would open when you knocked.

Going through to the kitchen, with its old-fashioned turquoise units and big American fridge, Natty enjoyed the fantasy that the house was hers.

Inspected closely, the interior bordered on the shabby. The floor tiles and painted woodwork bore the knocks of heavy use. But the casually distressed or 'patina'd' look was the latest trend on the vintage scene, and the house's big rooms and high ceilings retained a grandeur that a few tatty edges only enhanced. Compared to the cramped council house Natty had grown up in, it felt like a palace.

David Royale had a big kitchen, of course. But, like the rest of his airy West End flat, it was sleek, ultra-modern and full of gadgets Natty hadn't known existed — let alone how you worked them. Impressive as it had been to see how the truly rich lived, she'd never felt remotely at home there.

Exploring the cupboards, Natty remembered Margie's comment about tea and coffee being included in the rent, and Jase's interjection, 'Anything else, write your name on it!' Jude's private supply of muesli was clearly identified in black marker, with an exclamation mark after her name. Matt, she discovered, was a porridge man. A jumbo size box of cornflakes had no name on it, and Natty decided no one would mind if she helped herself to a bowl. She'd replace it later.

She'd just made tea and carried it to the breakfast bar when a car door slammed and the back door burst open.

'Aaaagh!' yelled Matt as a pile of ice-cream tubs tumbled out of his arms and clattered across the kitchen floor.

'Here, let me . . . ' Natty leapt off her stool to retrieve some of the tubs.

'No, it's okay, I've got them now!' Sweeping the tubs into the crook of his muscular arm, Matt dumped them onto the breakfast bar.

'You know how to make an entrance, I'll say that for you!' Natty said, as she added a final tub to the collection. Her heart was drumming, but it wasn't only the shock of Matt's all-action arrival that had put her in a fluster. With his biceps bulging like Popeye's from the sleeves of his gleaming white T-shirt, Matt was undoubtedly the most gorgeous man she'd ever seen. His puppy-like clumsiness only endeared him to her all the more. With his chiselled face set in a wide grin beneath his bright vanilla flat top, he radiated a positive energy that lifted her spirits like a sunny day.

'They're samples of a new line I'm

thinking of buying,' Matt explained. 'Try one — let me know what you think.'

Natty needed no encouragement.

'Blackberry Passion!' she read, before prising off the plastic lid. She dug in with her cornflake spoon and caught her breath as a chill froze her mouth and the flavour exploded on her tongue. 'Mmmmmm! Delicious! Buy it, buy it, buy it!'

'That's exactly what I was thinking!' Matt responded as he put the kettle on.

'So who's running the ice-cream parlour?' Natty asked, as she tucked into the ice cream.

'Oh, it's Jen's day. I only went in briefly to see the rep.'

Jen. The name gave Natty a little stab and she tried not to show any reaction. Last night, Matt had seemed so down, his meeting with his wife having apparently gone badly. So why did his description of their work arrangements sound so light and matter-of-fact?

Natty desperately wanted to ask him

about last night's meeting but, having known him such a short time, it seemed too forward.

'What are you up to today?' Matt asked, as he made himself some tea.

'I've got to go to my mum's to pick up some of my things.' Natty sighed, because although she couldn't wait to get her hands on her clothes, transporting them across town would be a chore. Her mum would probably be busy, so she'd have to get a cab, which she couldn't afford.

'Would you like a lift?' Matt offered.

'It must be my lucky day!' Natty replied. 'You're sure you've got time, though?'

'I've got an art lesson with Jude at two. We'll be back before then, won't we?'

'We will if we hurry!' Effortlessly Natty sprang off her stool. 'I'll get my suitcase!'

★　★　★

Margie's house had no garden, just a small paved yard at the back. As Natty went through the kitchen door she stopped dead in her tracks.

Parked diagonally across the yard was the car of her dreams — a 1957 four-door Chevrolet Bel Air.

Built like a tank that had visited a beauty parlour, the huge American car had white-wall tyres, a chrome front grille like a grinning shark and impressive tail fins.

The good looks didn't stop there. With a gleaming chrome pinstripe running along the side, the upper curves of the wings, bonnet and boot were finished in an eye-catching pale chalk dust pink. The roof and the lower half of the car were painted in a pale cream.

Splashed in red across the doors was a miniature version of the proud sign that stood above Matt's ice-cream parlour:

Matt's!
Ice Cream, Shakes, Coffee & Cakes
— Indulge yourself!

Screaming with delight, Natty ran around the vehicle, stroking its lustrous lacquered paint, barely believing it was real. She'd seen plenty of American cars at rockabilly festivals, of course — they were part and parcel of the retro scene. But she'd never believed she'd actually ride in one, let alone meet a guy who owned one.

Already as high in her estimation as she imagined a man could be, Matt leapt one gazillion points higher.

'Like it?' grinned Matt.

'Love it!' Reaching the passenger door, Natty wrapped her hand with relish around the big chrome handle, pushed the button with her thumb and pulled the door open with a squeak.

'Are you driving?' Matt asked in surprise.

'Er?' Natty asked blankly. She giggled as she realised that, being an American car, the big chrome and white steering wheel was where she expected the passenger side to be.

'Scoot over!' Matt instructed.

The car had a bench seat newly

reupholstered in bright pink and white. Bouncing onto the smooth leather in her vintage jeans, Natty slid across to the passenger side as Matt eased his big muscular frame behind the wheel.

'What a car!' Natty gazed around the spacious interior. Everything from the polka-dot roof lining to the chrome-rimmed dashboard looked brand new.

Matt turned the ignition key with an old-fashioned metallic screech that stroked something deep in Natty's soul. He pressed a chunky button in the dashboard and as Danny & The Juniors' 1958 hit *Rock'n'roll Is Here To Stay* filled the interior, Natty felt as if she was in a music video.

Matt stretched his arm around the back of the seat behind her as he looked over his shoulder to back into an alley at the rear of the house. He drove around into St George's Road and as he put his foot down, the engine let out the distinctive burbling sound that only mid-century American cars make. Natty squealed and patted the dashboard as if it were a living thing.

'What's her name?' she shouted above the music.

'Er . . . Chevy?' Matt replied, looking confused.

'No, her real name! Like Betsy or Pinky or something!'

'Rosie calls her the ice-cream van.'

'The ice-cream van it is then!' Natty squealed. She knew she was acting like a kid in Disneyland, but she didn't care. David's Lamborghini had been sleek, luxurious and heart-racingly fast. But a '57 Chevrolet — now that was what Natty called a car!

★ ★ ★

Northcliffe was a quiet, well-kept council estate built just after the war. The roads were wide and lined with trees, and the little brown brick terraced houses had neat privet hedges, although Natty noticed that every time she came home more and more of the hedges had been ripped out and replaced with driveways that were home to vans, caravans and boats.

'Nice car, mate!' called one of a bunch of ten-year-olds, interrupting their mid-street football match to let Matt turn into Natty's road.

Regally eyeing the kids through her Twinco sunglasses, Natty wished she'd be able to see the faces of her old neighbours, doubtless spying through their net curtains, when they saw her step out of Matt's dream car. She knew most of the estate's residents had always disapproved of her Hollywood dress sense, as if she had ideas above her station.

It was only in the high street, along the prom and in the little cobbled lanes full of cool boutiques, where the town's more colourful inhabitants gathered, that Natty had ever felt she fitted in. Yet, as a rebellious fifteen-year-old, the censorious looks she drew in her own part of town only added to the delight she took in walking out for the evening dressed as Betty Grable, with an air of superiority to match her heels and fox-fur cape.

'It's that one, over there on the right — the one with the animal ambulance on the drive!' Natty pointed. 'Mum's only mission in life is saving all the poor little animals of the world!'

'Nice house,' said Matt, as he parked in the shade of a tree.

Natty glanced at him, to see if he was being genuine, and wasn't really surprised to see that he was. It was strange, she thought, how comfortable she felt going to her mum's with Matt. She'd hardly ever taken a boyfriend home. Whenever she did, she'd felt ill at ease the whole time, as if the Natty who lived with her mum and dad and the Natty her friends knew occupied worlds that mixed as well as oil and water.

She certainly couldn't have taken David home — she would have died of embarrassment at the mere suggestion. It wasn't that she was ashamed of where she came from, but she knew instinctively that he would look down on it.

With Matt, she realised that for the

first time in her life the question of how he'd react to her parents' house had never crossed her mind. Although he'd grown up in a huge house with a flamboyant actress mother and a father who had been the biscuit king of England, she sensed that he didn't have a snobbish bone in his body.

She also realised that for the first time in her life, she was sitting next to a man she'd be proud to bring home and introduce as her boyfriend. He *wasn't* her boyfriend, of course. He was nothing like that, and may never be. But it gave her ego a tremendous boost to make-believe for a moment that he was.

Filled with warm feelings, Natty skipped from the car and opened the little wooden gate to her front path. Matt fetched her suitcase from the boot and followed her.

'Mother dear!' Natty sang, as she let herself into the hall. 'Natty's home!'

Her mother's red head glanced up from a text message she was reading while perched on a stool in the little kitchen at the end of the short hall.

'Oh, hello, Natalie.' Moira Smalls went back to thumbing her phone. 'I didn't know you were coming home.'

'You know me. Full of surprises!'

As Matt followed Natty into the cramped little space at the foot of the stairs, Moira glanced up again. She came down the hall, phone in hand, to take a look at him. Slim and make-up free, with her hair cut in a plain bob, Moira was wearing navy blue animal paramedic overalls and a belt heavy with a torch, radio and other equipment that, to Natty, always made her look halfway between a nurse and a cop.

'So is this the mysterious David . . . ?' Moira began, curiously.

'No. Matt's come to help me move some things over to my new . . . ' Natty stopped herself just in time. She almost said 'my new apartment,' which would have been much more impressive than 'room', but she couldn't lie in front of Matt.

' . . . my new place in St George's

Road!' Natty continued with barely a pause. At least the address was posh! 'I'm moving back into town!'

Her mum looked at her in confusion. 'I thought you and David were going to live in London.'

'Change of plan where David was concerned!' Natty said with a sigh. 'I broke it off.'

'Oh.' Her mum blinked at her in surprise.

Natty grinned weakly to hide her pain. Feeling suddenly small and vulnerable, she thought it would be nice if her mum hugged her at that point, although she would have been embarrassed in front of Matt if she had. They'd never been a huggy family.

Her mum looked ill at ease, the way her mum and dad always did when anything emotional cropped up. Natty was glad when Matt broke the awkward silence by thrusting out his hand.

'I'm Matt, by the way!'

'Although that's not his real surname!' Natty quipped.

'Pleased to meet you.' Moira gave Matt's big hand a cautious shake, barely touching it with the tips of her fingers and thumb. She turned back to her phone. 'I'm afraid you've caught me on the hop, Natalie. I've got an Alsatian with a broken leg to pick up from the pound and about a million emails to answer. Do you mind if you make yourself some tea? I've got to get my kit together.'

Natty watched with a familiar feeling of deflation as her mother went back down the hall, thumbing away at her phone. On one hand she was glad they weren't the sort of family that were always into each other's business. Natty was an only child who liked her privacy. She had no wish to air her embarrassment over the David Royale disaster, especially not in front of Matt.

But she did wish her mum had made a fuss of Matt. Or that she was impressed by Natty's new residence in the heart of town. Or that she could have taken her mum outside to ooh and ahh over the Chevy.

She reminded herself that she'd come home unannounced, and hadn't phoned in a month. She couldn't expect her mum to drop everything for her, especially when she was busy.

A hurt little girl's voice inside Natty said her mum was always busy. But then, she remembered brightly, she was busy herself.

'Follow me!' Natty said. She beckoned Matt with her finger and trotted up the narrow stairs.

On the small landing, three doors stood ajar. The fourth was closed and painted pink. On it was a cardboard star, eighteen inches across and covered in gold foil. Written across the star in silver glitter was the legend *Miss Natty Smalls*.

'Welcome to my dressing room!' Natty trilled. She fished out a key.

'You lock your bedroom?' Matt chuckled.

'I don't think of it so much as a bedroom, more like secure storage!' she explained.

Natty opened the door into darkness — she kept the curtains closed to stop the sun fading her delicate clothes — and clicked on the light.

'Wow!' Matt exclaimed. 'You could open a shop!'

Apart from the wardrobe and chests of drawers, all of which were filled to bursting, the room was jammed with free-standing clothes rails, every inch of which were crammed with vintage outfits. Many hung in dry cleaners' bags, with tantalising glimpses of satin, chiffon or sixty-year-old lace dangling from the bottom. The shoulders and sleeves of other garments gleamed with fiery silks, sequins or elaborate embroidery. Hats hung on the ends of the rails. Fur stoles and feather boas were draped over the top. More clothes hung from the picture rail and the outside edge of the wardrobe.

Edging sideways into what little floor space was left, to let Matt come into the room with her, Natty found her knees pressed hard against the side of her single bed, although it was barely recognisable as a bed. The lower half was covered in cardboard boxes filled with clothes and records. The pillows at the top end were hidden beneath a huddle of teddy bears, dolls and velvet horses, all of them lovingly looked after since her earliest childhood.

'I like your wallpaper!' grinned Matt.

What little wall wasn't hidden by hanging coats and dresses was covered with posters, magazine covers and photographs of Natty's heroes and heroines. Above her headboard was one of the iconic calendar shots of Marilyn Monroe, draped nude across a red velvet sheet in all her alabaster glory. To Natty it was the most beautiful celebration of femininity ever captured in a work of art.

Gazing smoulderingly at Marilyn from the opposite wall was the four-foot-tall face of a young Elvis. From every gap between the hanging clothes peeked a galaxy of rock'n'roll stars and Hollywood actresses. Alongside them posed the modern-day burlesque queens Immodesty Blaize and Dita Von Teese, whose retro glamour kept alive the tradition of women as goddesses.

'Look at these records!' Matt ran an admiring finger along the spines of the big cardboard LP sleeves. Excitedly, he pulled out one of the albums.

'Brenda Lee's first album from 1961!' Matt held the well-thumbed charity shop find with a reverence a philatelist would reserve for a Penny Black. He turned it over and exclaimed, 'It's got *I Just Want To Be Wanted* on it!'

Natty felt as if she were going to burst with pride — and a whole host of other emotions which were surging up so strongly within her that she didn't dare speak.

Matt was the first man she'd ever let into her room. In fact, she hadn't let anyone in since she was thirteen. If she had, she knew she would have been hopping about with irritation, not wanting them to touch or even look at anything. As a teenager, her room was her secret world. Now it was a box she kept her past in. The heroines who had shaped her, the glimpses of her childhood . . . it was all too private, too personal and too tender to be pawed or scoffed at by someone who wouldn't understand.

Inviting Matt into her most private space felt like an act of thrilling intimacy and trust. His presence felt so comfortable, she wanted to slam the door and never let him out!

Putting the record back carefully, Matt gazed in awe at the rails and rails of clothes. 'So how much are we taking back?'

'Just a few essentials,' Natty sang. 'Arms out!'

Matt held out his forearms, palms up, at waist height. Natty lifted a bag from one of the rails and laid it across his arms. She put another one on top, then another and another until he could barely get his chin on top of the pile.

'If you put those in the car to begin with, I'll be filling my case until you come back.'

While Matt staggered carefully down the stairs, Natty opened the first of her several underwear drawers and began packing some of the items she didn't want Matt to see. *Not yet anyway,* she thought with a minxish smile.

★ ★ ★

As they pulled into the yard at the back of Margie's house, the big Chevrolet was riding lower than usual on its soft springs thanks to a pile of clothes on the back seat that completely blocked the rear window. The boot was so full Matt had barely been able to close it.

'Do you mind if we unpack later?' said Matt, as he turned off the engine. 'It's almost time for my art lesson.'

'I'll unpack,' Natty assured him. 'You've done enough work for one day!'

Leaving her things in the car for the time being, they went into the kitchen where they were greeted by the delicious aroma of strong coffee. Jude was stirring a cafetière. With the sun striking golden highlights in her huge frizz of chocolate curls, the tall, willowy woman was wearing a pyjama-like outfit in red and gold silk that Natty thought looked quite cool.

'Coffee, you two?' Jude offered with a toothy grin.

'Yeah!' Matt gasped.

Natty felt guilty for not making him a cup of tea at her mum's.

'I'm sorry Mum was a bit offhand,' she apologised.

'Not at all. She was busy.' Matt shrugged good-naturedly.

'I wish I could remember a time when she wasn't,' Natty whispered, almost to herself.

She felt an extra stab of guilt for speaking negatively about her mother. It wasn't as if she'd ever had any conflict with her parents. In fact, she sometimes wished there *had* been some conflict, instead of the three of them leading such insular lives.

Her mum ran a calm, well-ordered home, but when she wasn't driving her animal ambulance, she worked for four or five charities. Her dad worked long overtime shifts on building sites. And little Natty had been left alone with her old records, her black and white films and her imagination.

To her surprise, Matt said, breezily, 'She reminds me of Mum. Always rushing off to her shop, or, in the old days, to make a biscuit advert, or organise one of her parties. As for Dad, well, he worked round the clock, really.'

Gazing away, with a sigh, the big muscular man momentarily looked like a lost little boy.

Natty gazed at him, intrigued. She found it hard to imagine feeling left out in a household headed by the flamboyant Margie. To Natty, having the Coconut Crunch girl for a mum would have been a dream childhood. At the very least, Matt's parents had shown him it was possible to make something of yourself.

'So when's your next gig?' Matt asked, as he pulled up a stool and sat at the breakfast bar.

'Gig?' Natty asked, distracted.

'You're a singer, aren't you?' Matt asked, eagerly.

Natty hesitated, caught off-guard. The admiring look in Matt's eyes as he gazed at her made it tempting to say she was. In other circumstances, she might have encouraged his delusion, but sharing a house with him would make the white lie a little hard to sustain.

'Ah, well, um . . . not exactly . . . not *professionally*,' Natty admitted, coquettishly.

'Really?' Matt looked taken aback. 'Well you should be! That song you were singing last night sounded fantastic!'

'You heard that?' Natty stammered, nervously.

'I loved it!' Matt enthused. 'Is it something you wrote?'

'Well, it's not quite finished yet . . . ' Natty began, shyly.

'It's brilliant!' said Matt, giving her his megawatt grin.

'What? You really think so?' Natty latched onto the compliment. She sat down across the breakfast bar from him, eager for more feedback. She'd never aired her songs in front of anybody before.

'I only heard it once and I've had that chorus going round in my head ever since!' Matt began to sing in a strong, tuneful voice, *'Everybody deserves a second chance . . . '*

Natty gazed at him in wonder. The sound of her words coming out of his mouth was such a strangely intimate thing that she wasn't sure what it was doing to her.

'That sounds interesting,' said Jude, bringing three mugs of coffee to the breakfast bar.

'Wait till you hear it!' Matt enthused. 'I mean, what a brilliant line. *Everybody deserves a second chance.* Who doesn't feel like that?'

'I certainly do,' Jude agreed. 'Jase and I were saying the same thing last night . . . '

'You really like it?' Natty pressed. At the same time she was thinking, *are you looking for a second chance, Matt?*

Matt leaned towards her, eagerly. 'There's this little club just opened on the seafront. They always have a spot for new songwriters. Why don't you come down and do a couple of songs, see how it goes?'

'Me?' Natty reeled from the suggestion. 'I couldn't! I mean, I've never . . . '

'Don't tell me you're shy!' Matt teased.

Natty giggled, because she knew the suggestion sounded ridiculous. With her orchid in her Fifties hairdo, her hip-hugging vintage jeans and her gingham shirt knotted under a bust shaped like two bullets, shy was the last thing Natty looked. But how things looked on the outside and how they felt on the inside weren't always the same.

Squirming on her stool, Natty confessed, 'Actually . . . I'd be terrified! I've never sung my songs in front of anyone, not even my mum and dad. Standing on stage and singing them in front of a bunch of strangers . . . I'd die of embarrassment!'

'It's a really retro place,' Matt enthused. 'All the rockabilly crowd go there. They have rock'n'roll, jiving

. . . you'll love it.'

Natty was tempted. Of course she wanted to be on stage. Who didn't? Every time she picked up her guitar and sang in the privacy of her bedroom she imagined herself walking onto an arena stage to face, with utter poise, the glare of the spotlights and the adulation of an audience that stretched into the infinite distance. She'd never thought she'd do it for real, though. And shyness was only part of the reason.

Natty thought of her lyrics not so much as songs to be performed or recorded, but as entries in a diary — it was how she worked out her feelings. And who wanted to stand on stage and reveal their deepest feelings?

'Say you'll come!' Matt pressed.

Natty gazed into his pleading blue eyes and realised with a jolt that he wasn't just suggesting she share her songs with the world — he was asking her out! The prospect of an evening alone with Matt was a completely different thing. The fact they could both pretend it wasn't a date at all, but something more casual, meant she didn't even have to worry about the complications of his life with Jen.

'I guess I'm just a girl who can't say no!' Natty giggled.

She was instantly glad she'd said yes — to the going out with Matt part, anyway. That felt perfectly right, like something that was meant to be. But as for the going on stage part, Natty wondered what she was getting herself into. She may have crossed a private barrier by letting Matt see the intimate secrets of her room. But baring her soul to a roomful of strangers was a scarier thing altogether.

4

'Nice look!' called the newspaper seller as Natty click-clacked past his kiosk in her gleaming black stilettos.

'Thanks!' Even for a girl who always made an effort, Natty had pulled out all the stops. Channelling Manhattan millionaire business woman circa 1959, she was wearing her oatmeal wool pencil dress, tight at the knee and belted like a wasp at her girdled waist. The dress was high-necked and sleeveless, and she'd covered her upper arms with a silk scarf in a luscious shade of lemon, holding the scarf in place with a topaz brooch in a silver setting.

She'd pulled her ruby-red hair into a bun on the back of her head and, atop her crown, pinned at a jaunty angle, a dinky little pillbox hat matched her dress. As a final note of sophistication, a little net veil danced over her forehead, with tiny black hearts woven into it to match the ones in her fishnet stockings.

For accessories she wore white elbow-length gloves with her late grandmother's silver wristwatch fastened over the top, and she carried a large red leather purse which she'd found in a charity shop and polished up to look like new.

'Going to a wedding?' the news vendor called after her.

'Hopefully one day!' Natty trilled over her shoulder.

But at that moment, she had more pressing matters on her mind. Singing a few songs in a rockabilly club may be the first step to superstardom, but she doubted it would pay her rent in the short term. Natty Smalls needed a job, and it was time to test her theory that dressing to kill would open any door.

Twenty minutes later, Natty was walking daintily up the steps of the regional television centre — dainty being the only sort of movement that a tight-at-the-knee hemline and three-inch stiletto heels allowed.

At the top of the sun-drenched steps, a uniformed security guard leaped into action and held open a smoked glass door.

Well, so far so good! thought Natty, as she swept past the first hurdle.

The glass doors opened into a sunny, marble-floored atrium that extended about a mile to a sleek reception desk. Along the side walls were a couple of green designer couches and a scattering of miniature palm trees in big terracotta pots. The air conditioning was as cold as ice.

Now this was the sort of place a girl should work! Taking a deep breath, she forced herself to make the long walk to the desk as slowly and classily as possible. She imagined it was a long tracking shot in a movie, with the camera lingering on her seductively swaying hips the way it follows Marilyn Monroe's shapely rear in the opening scene of *Niagara*.

As Natty neared the desk, her heart began to quicken, but she was determined not to be intimidated.

Behind the desk sat a model-thin woman with expensively groomed blonde hair and a dark red designer dress. The receptionist looked up with a quizzically raised eyebrow.

'May I help you?'

Natty looked down with regal disdain and said in her poshest voice, 'Natty Smalls. I've come to see Robin Greenbaum — the news editor.'

There were many aspects of twenty-first century life that Natty had no fondness for. She was probably the only girl of her generation who didn't possess a mobile phone, on the grounds that all her heroines from the Forties and Fifties had got along more than happily without one. They'd certainly have been far too classy to reveal the intimate trivialities of their lives on anything so vulgar as Twitter or Facebook. In Natty's book, being distant and unavailable was a vital ingredient of feminine allure.

She'd felt particularly pleased about her phone-less state in the days since leaving London, because it meant

David had absolutely no way of contacting her or finding out where she was. But she had to give credit to the usefulness of the internet in coughing up the names of important people. Natty had done an hour of research on the free computer in the library earlier that morning.

The expensively groomed receptionist frowned at a diary on her desk and asked, coldly, 'Is he expecting you?'

Natty feigned surprise. 'Don't tell me he's forgotten?'

'Hmmm.' The receptionist regarded her with suspicion and picked up her phone. 'Hi Fran, I have a Natty Smalls in reception who'd like to see Robin.'

The receptionist listened a moment, then glanced up at Natty. 'Mr Greenbaum's PA has asked me what you wish to see him in connection with?'

Natty hesitated briefly, then said, 'The senior reporter's job, of course!'

The receptionist relayed the information into the phone. She listened again, then put down the phone with a self-satisfied simper. 'Mr Greenbaum's PA says we have no vacancies at present, but if you'd care to write in with your CV, we'll gladly put your application on file.'

Natty inwardly deflated, but was determined not to show it. Before she turned to make the mile-long walk of shame back to the smoked glass doors, she asked lightly, 'Do you have many applications on file?'

The receptionist pushed back her chair on casters and tugged open a yard-long filing cabinet drawer rammed solid with paper. With a relish Natty couldn't help thinking was a little unnecessary, the girl declared, 'This is the file!'

As Natty walked down the TV station steps, she began to wonder if her plan had a flaw. She had no doubt that anyone who saw her would find her suitable for a job in front of the cameras, but what if you couldn't get anyone to actually see you? She wasn't too downhearted, though. Natty believed in starting at the top and working her way down, and there were quite a few more doors to knock on.

As she sauntered into the local radio station, Natty's spirits lifted immediately. The receptionist sat with her back to a glass wall through which Natty could see the dozen or more occupants of a busy newsroom, and that meant they could see her, too!

As the receptionist phoned through her request, Natty's eagle eye saw a youngish man with a thick mop of curly hair pick up the phone on his desk. That had to be the man the receptionist was speaking to! Confirming Natty's intuition, the man turned and looked sharply at her through narrow designer glasses.

Quickly, Natty looked nonchalantly away and struck her most starry posture — chin up, eyebrows arched, scarlet lips pouting, girdle and bullet bra doing the work that modern undergarments could only dream of.

The receptionist put down her phone with a smile. 'You're in luck, Miss Smalls. Mr Longman says he's got five minutes if you'd like to go through.'

As Natty stepped through the glass door, the buzzing atmosphere of the newsroom thrilled her. It was just like the movies! Men in ties and shirt sleeves were tapping urgently at computer keyboards or talking quickly into phones. Young interns were weaving between desks carrying sheaves of paper. Phones bleeped. Printers whirred. At the back of the room, behind a further glass wall, a woman in headphones was actually reading the news on air!

Rhys Longman strode towards her in a shiny suit, with his hand outstretched. He was aptly named, thought Natty as he was the tallest, thinnest man she'd ever seen. With his thick mop of curly hair and narrow specs, he only looked a few years older than she was. His youth added to her optimism. In a couple of years, Natty Smalls would be running this place!

'So, Miss Smalls,' Longman grinned. 'I hear you want to be a top reporter? Well, you've got the right attitude, knocking on doors. Come and sit down.'

He led her to a small booth at the side of the news room. 'What experience have you had?'

'Well,' Natty said slowly. 'Not experience as such . . . '

'Hospital radio? Student radio?' he asked encouragingly.

'I listen to the radio!' Natty stated with a winning smile.

Longman laughed and Natty got the feeling she was doing quite well.

'What did you think of the opening heads on the breakfast news this morning?'

Natty cocked her ear, as if Longman had unexpectedly started speaking Chinese. 'The, er . . . ?'

'The opening heads — the headlines?' Longman prompted. 'And the two-way in the second lead? Do you think it worked?'

Two-way? Second lead? Natty didn't have a clue what he was talking about.

'I, um, didn't actually hear the news

this morning,' Natty finally admitted.

'You didn't?' Longman frowned. 'O-kay. Suppose you had two minutes to interview 3-Dom, the biggest band in the country at the moment. What would you ask them?'

Natty thought hard before offering, 'Why do they think everyone likes them so much?'

Longman laughed. 'Anything else?'

Natty racked her brain. She'd heard of 3-Dom, of course. The grinning girl group were plastered over every bus stop billboard and their romantic antics with various soap stars filled the papers on a daily basis. But as someone who seldom played any records recorded later than 1960, she had to admit, 'They're not really my kind of music.'

Longman smiled sympathetically, then stood up and offered his hand again.

'Well, thanks for coming into the station, Natty. I think you've got a really big future in radio ahead of you . . . '

'You do?' Natty exclaimed, excitedly.

' . . . but I think your first step should

be to get a bit more experience. I'd advise you to do one of the broadcast journalism courses, try some voluntary work on a community station then maybe come back and see me in a couple of years.'

As he showed her to the door, Longman added as an afterthought, 'You could always try getting some basic reporting experience on the local paper.'

Natty grinned with increasingly false optimism. 'That's exactly where I was heading next!'

Sadly, the response from the regional daily paper was just as bad. Having been taken all the way to a top floor office with breathtaking views over the town centre rooftops and scintillating ocean beyond, a stern middle-aged editor recommended she get an English degree then, after three years — Natty almost fainted at the thought of how old she'd be in three years' time — apply for a postgraduate course in journalism. After which he *might* consider her for a trainee position.

Natty left the office feeling drained. She wanted nothing more than a consolation sundae in Matt's ice-cream parlour. In fact, she longed for just the sight of Matt's grinning, square-jawed, chisel-cheeked face. What she wouldn't give to sink exhausted and tearful into his muscular arms at that very moment!

Natty had never been convinced that whimpering and tearful was a look that worked for her, though, and she couldn't face Matt in such a disheartened mood. The last thing she wanted was Matt's sympathy — she wanted his admiration. When she left the house that morning Natty had promised herself that before the day was through, she'd burst triumphantly into Matt's to announce her new job as Ace Reporter Natty Smalls!

Natty had one more place on her list to try — the weekly local rag. Thankfully for her aching feet, it was right across the road from the big paper. Held upright by little more than the supportive hug of her girdle, Natty took a deep breath, gathered what was left of her hopes and pushed open the door.

On the threshold, Natty stopped dead. In contrast to the plush modern offices she'd visited so far, the reception area was . . . interesting. With scuffed — and in a couple of places missing — tiles on the floor, wood panelling with a long-dulled finish and cream upper walls stained with nicotine, it looked like a set from a 1950s film noir and didn't appear to have been dusted for several years.

Natty felt perfectly at home in her Fifties oatmeal pencil dress, pillbox hat, little net veil and stockings, as if she were walking into an old photograph. Beginning to feel just the teeniest bit more optimistic, she sauntered up to a big oak reception desk behind which a portly man with steel-grey hair and a silk-backed waistcoat was sorting some bundles of newspapers on a wide shelf along the back wall.

On the desk sat a brass service bell.

Natty took great delight in giving it a loud ding with the palm of her white-gloved hand.

The portly man with the waistcoat turned slowly and gave her a level look over his half glasses. Natty guessed he was probably a few years overdue for retirement.

'Can I help you?' the man asked, unsmiling.

'Is the editor in?' Natty asked sweetly.

'You're looking at him.' The man looked her up and down.

Caught off-guard, Natty readied herself to put on the show of confidence she'd displayed in the previous offices. But suddenly she found she didn't have the energy to fake it. Sagging against the desk, she pleaded, 'I don't suppose you've got any jobs going, have you?'

The editor eyed her curiously, as if she'd just walked in from the set of an old movie, which she had to admit was exactly what she looked like. The editor looked rather as if he was in an old movie himself.

At length, a grandfatherly twinkle came into the newsman's eye. 'As a matter of fact, I have . . . '

★ ★ ★

Natty burst excitedly into Matt's ice-cream parlour and cried, 'I think a Matt's Sundae Special on the house is in order!'

Natty struck a hands on hips pose like Marilyn Monroe in *Some Like It Hot*. She froze as she realised the ice-cream seller wasn't Matt. It was a tall, slim woman with a sleek black ponytail — Matt's wife, Jen!

'Do I know you?' Jen narrowed her eyes, suspiciously.

'Um, is Matt in?' Natty squeaked.

Jen eyed her closely, and Natty wondered if Jen remembered her from the other day. Jen hadn't been in the parlour two minutes, but Natty's Fifties clothes and ruby-red hairstyle tended to stick in people's minds.

'He'll be here at two,' Jen answered, coldly.

Natty glanced at the metal rimmed clock with Marilyn Monroe's face. It was ten to.

'I'll come back!'

She turned around just as the bell jangled above the door. She almost walked smack into Matt. Wearing his usual tight white T-shirt and vintage black jeans, he was holding his four-year-old daughter Rosie high in his muscle-bound arms.

'Whoa!' Matt exclaimed as he and Natty almost collided. 'Hi, Natty! Great dress! How's the job-hunting?'

He looked over her shoulder and suddenly looked guilty. 'Oh, er, hi, Jen!'

Seeing the colour fall from Matt's face, Natty spun around in time to see Jen's face redden.

'So that's what this is about!' Jen came angrily around the counter. 'You told me there was no one else!'

'There wasn't!' Matt spluttered. 'I mean, there isn't!'

'I think there's some mistake . . . ' Natty began, weakly.

'Yes, mine — for trusting this rat!' Jen

stormed. 'Well, you can have your divorce! But if you think you're getting the house or this place you've got another thing coming! Come here, Rosie, we're going home!'

Jen snatched her daughter from Matt's arms and the infant began bawling.

'I'm only staying at Matt's mum's . . .' Natty began.

But Jen had already barged from the parlour. The bell jangled and the door slammed in her wake. In shock, Natty watched Jen's raven ponytail fly past the window, with Rosie's red and screwed up face screaming over her mother's shoulder.

At the tables, half a dozen yummy mummies and their sticky-faced offspring looked on agog, as if watching a soap opera.

Red-faced, Matt forced a shell-shocked grin and went to the jukebox. He pressed a couple of chunky buttons and Bill Haley's *Rock Around The Clock* filled the stunned silence, bringing some semblance of normality back to the ice-cream parlour. As the customers made a polite show of returning to their own business, Matt went behind the counter and sat down with a heavy sigh.

Cringing with embarrassment, Natty slunk up to the counter.

'I'm so sorry if I've messed things up . . .'

Matt shrugged and gave her a weak grin. 'Not your fault, Natty. Sadly, it's been like this between me and Jen for the past three years.'

Natty leaned her folded arms on the counter and stroked the back of her stockinged calf with the toe of her court shoe. Keeping her voice low to preserve some confidentiality, she said, 'You've been trying to make it work, though?'

Matt rubbed the back of his neck. 'We talked about a divorce the other night. We should have called it a day years ago. But with Rosie it's difficult. Plus Jen has a half share in this place. Not the best reason for staying together, I know, but when we opened it, I thought it would be forever.'

Matt looked away. He looked suddenly

broken and Natty's heart ached for him. She imagined what it must be like to live in a loveless marriage for as long as he and Jen had, constantly trying to stick a plaster over the chasm between them for the sake of their child and business. She marvelled at how Matt generally managed to look so cheerful and concluded he must have a heart of pure gold.

Softly, she said, 'Maybe a clean break would actually be better for Rosie. You know, less tension between you and Jen.'

Matt's eyes searched hers, looking for . . . for what? Natty wondered. Answers? Strength? Reassurance? Love?

The last thought suddenly scared Natty. Matt needed more than a happy ending. He was a man with three years of a bad marriage behind him and a divorce in front of him. He had a daughter who not only needed him but needed a stepmother, too. Then there was Jen — who would be in Matt's life forever, whatever happened, because she was Rosie's mother.

Matt needed more than romance, Natty realised. He needed commitment, support, stability, a mother to his child. Being with him wouldn't be a fairytale, it wouldn't be easy, and neither could it be for anything less than forever. If she led him on and promised what she couldn't deliver, Natty realised she wouldn't just be playing with her own heart, she'd be playing with lives that had already-been hurt a great deal. At twenty-one, Natty wondered whether she was strong enough to take on the task.

'Anyway,' Matt was saying. 'How's the job-hunting?'

'Em?' Natty asked distractedly. Compared to the scale of the events unfolding in Matt's life, Natty's success that morning no longer felt as important as it had when she'd burst into the ice-cream parlour.

'Any luck?' Matt prompted. The keen interest in his eyes rekindled Natty's sense of achievement. She also sensed that he wanted to talk about anything that would take his mind off his own woes. Which meant a little showing-off wouldn't just be excusable, it was the very least she could do to help him!

Posing theatrically, Natty fluttered her eyelashes with false modesty and said lightly, 'Oh, I just walked into the local paper, sweet-talked the editor . . . and he gave me a job on the spot!'

'You just asked for a job and they gave it to you?' Matt beamed at her in admiration.

'Starting this very afternoon!'

'You are amazing, Natty!'

'I try to be!' Natty laughed.

'So you're an ace reporter now?'

'Well, not exactly,' Natty confessed. 'It turned out his receptionist has gone on maternity leave, so he's given me a job answering the phones and manning the desk in the lobby. But many top reporters start out doing less, and he told me that if I come across any news stories I should certainly let him know!'

'This deserves a Matt's Sundae Special on the house!' said Matt, leaping to his feet.

'That's exactly what I said when I came in!' Natty agreed.

'All the trimmings?' Matt said as he reached for a tall glass.

'Every one!' Natty said emphatically.

'Actually, it's a double celebration,' said Matt, beaming, as he began spooning strawberries and peaches into the glass. 'Because I've just been round to see Justin at The Cinderella Club. I told him how great your song is and he's put you on the bill tomorrow night!'

5

For her stage debut, Natty went for the full-on rock'n'roll look with a black swirl skirt that flared wide at the knee above a frothy explosion of ivory silk and lace petticoats. The skirt had a chain of four-inch embroidered red roses around the hem. The blooms were matched by three on each breast of a black velvet waistcoat that she wore over a cream satin shirt closed at the throat by a bolo string tie with a mother-of-pearl clasp set in a delicate silver surround.

She completed the outfit with two items she'd bought in her lunch hour specially for the occasion — a large and delicately fragrant pink rose, which she pinned above her left ear, and a pair of sheer black stockings with a seamed back and a pattern of little black musical notes. She further decorated he stockings with a pair of frilly garters adorned with white silk bows.

As she adjusted the garters on her thighs, Natty smiled at the thought of the effect they'd have on Matt if he walked in at that moment. Not that she had any intention of him seeing them. The frisson she got from such details came not from displaying them, but from the secret knowledge that they were there.

As she dropped the hem of her skirt into place, a rap on the door made her jump.

'Are you ready, Natty?' called Matt.

'Ready, willing and waiting!' Natty pulled open the door.

'Wow!' said Matt. 'You look fantastic!'

'I try my best!'

Natty went to grab her guitar case from the bed. Matt dived past her. 'Allow me!'

'You're a true gentleman!' Natty chirped.

'I try my best!' Turning to grin at her

as he left the room, Matt accide.
jammed the guitar case sideways acro.
the doorframe with a jolt that nearly
pulled his arm out of its socket. As the
case banged against the woodwork,
the guitar strings inside let out a
vibrating brangggg!

Natty gasped and Matt looked
mortified. Luckily it was a strong case
and the guitar was well-cushioned.

'Perhaps I'd better carry it?' Natty
ventured, nervously.

Matt clutched the case upright to his
body. 'No, I'll be careful. I'm just
nervous, I guess!'

'No more than I am!' Natty chimed
as she followed him onto the landing.

She'd secretly begun to revel in the
idea of making her first public perfor-
mance, but now they were actually
about to leave the house her heart was
pounding. That the gig was also her
first date with Matt only added to
her anxiety.

Clattering down the stairs after Matt,
she hummed the melody of her song

aloud, hoping she wouldn't forget the words.

As she slammed the front door behind them and stood at the top of the steps to the pavement, Natty's heart lifted once more at the sight of the Chevrolet parked at the kerb. If that wasn't a car to make a girl feel like a star, Natty didn't know what was.

While Matt put her guitar case in the boot, she skipped around to the passenger door. As she bounced onto the pink and white leather seat, her lungs filled with perfume and she noticed for the first time that Jude, Jase and Margie were squeezed together on the back seat.

'We thought you'd like a fan club for your first big night!' Margie beamed.

'Wouldn't miss it!' Jase gave her a double thumbs-up.

'Well, there's nothing on telly!' Jude grinned.

'I'm so glad you could come!' Natty meant it. It would be reassuring to know at least four people would be cheering her on, even if no one else was. At the same time, she couldn't help thinking, ruefully, *So much for a cosy date with Matt!*

Matt flopped in behind the wheel and pulled his door shut with a clunk. 'Well, this is the part of the journey I always enjoy — the moment I can tell you all to belt up!'

As Natty clicked her belt into place, Matt started the engine and rolled the big white-wall tyres off the kerb.

'Put some music on!' Margie urged.

'Yeah!' Natty agreed. Twisting round in her seat to grin at her landlady, she noticed Margie was wearing a white leather biker jacket over a low-cut lace blouse, a knee-length leather skirt with a fringed hem and white cowboy boots.

'I love your outfit!' Natty cried.

'Us girls have to keep our appearances up!' Margie replied, plumping up her enormous blonde bouffant.

Natty tried to imagine her own mother wearing such an outfit, let alone carrying it off with such aplomb. Once again, she envied Matt for having such a cool mum. She hoped Margie would be in her life forever.

Matt pressed a chunky button in the chrome-trimmed dashboard. Little Richard's exuberant voice and explosive piano filled the spacious interior and all five of the occupants spontaneously began singing along.

It was only a few minutes drive down the high street and along the prom, but it was without doubt the most exciting car trip Natty had ever made. Sitting in her rock'n'roll skirt and froth of petticoats, with Matt at the wheel in his leather biker jacket, she felt as if she'd fallen through a time warp into the era she'd always wished she'd been born in.

To share her life with a man like Matt was almost beyond her dreams. But to share it with a man like Matt and a car like this . . . well, that would be like winning the Lottery!

As Matt pulled up on the seafront Natty felt like a queen arriving in her carriage.

Jumping out, she breathed in deeply the cool and salty sea air and the smell of fish and chips. They were outside a big art deco pub with a flat roof and curved brick corners. Beside the main entrance was a separate doorway beneath a red neon sign that spelled The Cinderella Club.

A red glow filled the open doorway and rockabilly music drifted out to compete with the seagulls and passing traffic.

A 1950s American pick-up truck was parked in front of the Chevy with its bonnet up. Three guys with greased hair, leather jackets and turned-up jeans were poring over the engine. A couple of low-riding Harley Davidson motorbikes were parked on the pavement.

'All right, Matt?' called one of the greasers. Matt waved as he took Natty's guitar case from the boot of the Chevy.

Natty swayed her skirt in time with the music and thought, *This is my kind of place!*

Two rockabilly chicks were lounging near the doorway to the club in denim pedal pushers and singlets that showed off bare arms sleeved in multi-coloured tattoos. Their hair was worn in elaborate quiffs, and dyed pink and yellow like candyfloss.

'Hi, Matt!' the girls called in harmony.

'Evening, ladies!' Matt grinned.

Natty promptly crooked a proprietorial arm through Matt's and was gratified to see the faces of the two girls drop.

The doorway opened onto a narrow descending stairway. Natty followed Matt down with Margie's cowboy boots clomping along behind her and Jase and Jude bringing up the rear. At the foot of the stairwell they were met by a muscular guy with a shaven head and pebble glasses who was wearing a white singlet and white and grey camouflage trousers.

'Hey, Justin, my man!' Matt held out his hand cheerfully.

'Matt, darling!' Justin shook Matt's

hand in both of his and glanced further up the stairs to Margie. 'Ahh. And the Coconut Crunch girl!'

'Don't let the crumbs give you away!' Margie whispered huskily. She preened her blonde bouffant and blew Justin a theatrical kiss.

Justin's pebble glasses flashed as his eyes fell on Natty. 'And this must be your wonderful new girlfriend, Matt!'

Matt turned scarlet and looked as if he wanted the ground to swallow him. Justin gave him a friendly elbow in the stomach and reached past him to take Natty's hand. He kissed the back of her fingers with a loud 'Mwah!'

'Natty, my darling! I'm so pleased to meet you! Come in, come in! I've saved you all a table at the front.'

Justin swept aside a velvet curtain and led them into what at first appeared total darkness. They were met by a hearty round of applause and cheers, although it wasn't for them.

Unable to see much else of the basement room through the inky black,

Natty saw that just beside the entrance was a small stage framed with red drapes. Bathed in spotlights, a beefy middle-aged man with a handlebar moustache and long blond hair was rising from a stool. With rhinestones flashing like fish scales on his cowboy shirt, he un-strapped his guitar and acknowledged the warm reception with the languid wave of an old pro.

Justin squeezed Natty's hand and leaned close. 'Are you ready to go straight on, my darling?'

Natty looked at him agape. She'd expected a long wait until it was her turn to sing. She realised, though, that waiting around would only give her time to get more and more nervous. It was better to get this over with before she had time to chicken out.

'No time like the present!' Natty said confidently. Taking her guitar case from Matt she handed her heart-shaped handbag to Margie for safe-keeping. 'Wish me luck, guys!'

'Go get 'em, girl!' urged Margie.

Justin grasped Natty's hand and led her up the single step to the small, brightly lit stage. With hardly any headroom beneath the club's low ceiling, the heat from a bank of spotlights was intense.

The back wall of the stage was hung with a midnight-blue curtain dotted with bright white Christmas lights that twinkled like stars. Splashed across the star-scape was a red neon sign that reminded patrons they were in The Cinderella Club.

Some instruments — a double bass, drums, a guitar — and their cases were casually propped beneath the sign. Natty unpacked her guitar and left the case with the others. She plugged into the club's amplifier and gave the strings a tentative strum. The chord resounded through the club and the vibration of the strings went through Natty like a beautiful shiver.

For a moment Natty thought some-one had begun keeping steady but urgent time on a bass drum. Then she realised the thumping was her heart.

At the front of the stage, Justin moved the previous singer's stool to one side and went to the microphone. With the spotlights gleaming off his shaven head and flashing in his glasses, he beamed at the audience.

'Well, my rockabilly cats and kittens, I hope that set by our old friend the Birmingham Cowboy, Wes Stevens, has left you all purring with contentment. Very soon we'll be bringing on stage our headliners, Duke and the Bop Tones. But first, my darlings, as you all know, we like to be the first to bring you the best of new talent here in The Cinderella Club and this evening is no exception. Please give a warm welcome to one local Cinderella who will definitely be going to the ball . . . Miss Natty Smalls!'

At a table in front of the stage, Margie shrieked, whooped and clapped like a sea-lion. Matt, Jude and Jase cheered and applauded just as enthusiastically and, spurred by the noise, some other people in the club whistled and cheered, too.

Glad of the supportive hug of her girdle to keep her upright, Natty took a deep breath and hiked her lips into her biggest grin. She stepped into the glare of the spotlights with every nerve in her body tingling. Every day of her life Natty dressed to be seen and never had she been so perfectly showcased as she was within the spot-lit frame of The Cinderella Club's small stage.

Dressed to the nines, Natty felt as glamorous as rockabilly pioneer Rose Maddox stepping on to the stage of Nashville's Grand Ole Opry in 1954. With her pink rose in her ruby hair, the light flashing off the polished face of her Gretsch guitar, and her petticoats rippling like a foamy ocean below the hem of her swirl skirt, she knew she looked good. Whether she sounded good, she guessed she was about to find out!

Too nervous to speak, Natty began strumming her four chord intro. Plugged into the club's amplifier and coming out through the speakers, the guitar sounded completely different to the way it sounded when played un-amplified in her bedroom. The instrument felt as if it had come alive in her hands. The strings rang and jangled brightly and boldly. The notes reverberated and echoed around the room. More than a single instrument, the electrified guitar sounded like a full band. The music coming from her fingers sounded like the intro to a classic country-rock record by The Byrds.

The sound thrilled Natty. Her heart in her throat, she played the intro through twice to gather her confidence before putting her rose bud lips close to the microphone.

'I've been talking to the man upstairs . . . ' Her soprano voice, coming loud and clear through the speakers, sounded higher and drier to her than usual. But as she sang the second line, she began to relax and her tone gained depth.

'Telling him about all my worries and cares . . . '

Taking a deep breath to calm herself while she strummed the chords between the lines, Natty's eyes adjusted to the glare of the spotlights and she began to see more of the room beyond. Although she still couldn't see anybody clearly, she could discern the shapes of a lot of rock'n'roll hairdos on men and women alike. They were her kind of people and she could tell that they were watching with appreciation.

As she sang the third line, with a smile growing on her lips, a sudden thought went through Natty like a bolt of lightning from head to toe — *Natty Smalls, you can do this!*

Swinging her hand through the air with a flourish she struck the dramatic chord that led to the bridge and turned to Matt, who was watching with wide-eyed admiration from a table just in front of her knees. Wiggling her hips coquettishly, and swirling her petticoats around the musical notes in her stockings, Natty sang the line straight at him.

'*And then I saw you and my heart*

began to dance!' Natty paused. *'Could this really be our second chance?'*

Matt's mouth fell open and Natty let out a giggle that bubbled up from her very soul. The unscripted addition fitted the song perfectly and several people in the audience picked up on it, chuckling warmly and clapping as Natty stormed into the chorus.

'Everybody deserves a second chance . . . yeah, yeah, yeah!'

Natty ended the song with a sexy little electric guitar sting she'd been practising. For a second there was silence. Then the room exploded in cheers, applause and stamping feet.

Natty gave the crowd a flirty wave and a flick of her heel as she un-strapped her guitar. Justin barred her way from the stage. 'One more, my darling!' he urged.

'I've only rehearsed one!' Natty admitted.

'Then sing it again!' Matt hollered.

'Yeah!' encouraged a couple of voices from deep within the inky darkness.

Enjoying herself now, Natty did as she was asked and as she closed the song for the second time, everyone in the club sprang noisily to their feet. Natty blew them a farewell kiss and, at the same time, kissed goodbye to her mascara — black streaks of joy were whooshing down her cheeks like Niagara Falls.

Stowing her guitar at the back of the stage, Natty stepped off the stage into Matt's powerful arms. Clamping her stomach to his chest, he swung her around in a circle.

'Natty, you were wonderful!'

Natty screamed as the club whirled around her. Slithering back to the ground, she closed her mouth just in time to receive the warmest and most spontaneous kiss that had ever been bestowed upon her lips. The contact was electrifying and she knew she'd never forget the taste for as long as she lived.

Natty didn't have long to savour the moment, though. As she blinked and gazed into Matt's admiring eyes, Margie seized her in a hug of her own. Jude and Jase took their turns to congratulate her, too. Finally emerging from their arms, Natty felt as if her body was on fire and she suddenly realised she was experiencing a make-up failure of seismic proportions!

Fanning herself, Natty quipped, 'You'll have to excuse me while I go and compose myself!'

Bursting into the stark light and comparative cool of the ladies, Natty gripped the edge of the vanity unit and grinned at her reflection. Her senses were on overload and she felt as if her brain was about to explode. The cheers! The applause! Matt's hug! His kiss! She'd never seen her make-up in such disarray — and she'd never been on a greater high in her life!

* * *

Twenty minutes later, her nerves still jangling and her skin still tingling but

134

her face restored to artistic perfection, Natty returned to the club to find a three-piece rockabilly band, dressed in tartan drape jackets, were setting up their snare drum and double bass on stage.

Matt, Margie, Jude and Jase were standing around their table, talking animatedly. Justin was with them, along with a man Natty had never seen before. In perfect silhouette against the lights of the stage, the stranger was wearing a long drape jacket, carrying a shot glass, and had a quiff that jutted out above his forehead like the figurehead on a ship.

'Natty, my darling!' Justin enthused. 'There's a gentleman here who'd like to meet you.'

The stranger turned around and in the shifting light, Natty saw a pale but handsome face that could have been anywhere between thirty and forty-five. He had thick black eyebrows, eyes the colour of storm clouds, hair as black and slickly oiled as Elvis and a

Presley-style dimpled chin to match.

'Cameron Swoon,' the newcomer introduced himself, unsmiling, in the smooth dark Scottish burr of a young Sean Connery. He held out his hand, as if to shake. Instead he swivelled his thumb against his forefinger and produced a business card from nowhere, like a conjuror.

'That's a neat trick!' Natty said, as she took the card. The card listed just Swoon's name, the words 'Management Services' and a mobile phone number, but Natty barely glanced at it. There was an aura of self-confidence about Cameron Swoon that made her feel quite nervous and strangely excited at the same time.

Taking a moment to fully appraise him, Natty saw that Cameron was immaculately dressed in a black three-piece drape suit with a faint grey pinstripe. His crisp white shirt collar was closed with a neatly knotted black ribbon tie and a gold watch chain crossed the front of his waistcoat.

Most people didn't understand the Teddy Boy look, Natty reflected. They always pictured the cartoon-like primary colour drape jackets that Showaddywaddy popularised in the Seventies. The true 1950s-style Teds favoured the sombre colours, rich wool cloths and expensive tailoring of an Edwardian gentleman. Cameron Swoon understood the look completely and Natty had never seen a man wear it so well.'

He gave her the slightest of smiles, barely a flicker of movement in the left-hand corner of his mouth. In his low Scottish burr, he said, 'I'm no' gonna spin you a line about making you a star, Natty, but I have a friend who I think would be very interested in your music. Shall we sit down?'

Cameron pulled back a chair and nodded for Natty to take it. With Matt and the others gathering around curiously, Cameron pulled up another chair and sat in front of her.

'Do ye ken a record producer called Gary Morris?' Cameron asked quietly.

'Well, you've heard of 3-Dom, I know.'

'Who hasn't?' Natty said, remembering her interview at the radio station. She still didn't know anything about the girl group's music, but they were obviously the name on everybody's lips at the moment.

'This is completely confidential,' Cameron said in a low voice, 'but Gary developed 3-Dom from nothing and now they've taken off he's looking for a new act to nurture. I happen to know he's looking for someone with a bit more street cred, an artist who writes their own songs. He really likes the retro scene and I think you could be exactly what he's looking for.'

'Really?' Natty squealed.

'Gary's holding open auditions in London next month,' Cameron confirmed. 'But if you've got a CD, I could put it in his hand tomorrow and you'd be right at the front of the queue.'

'A CD?' Natty repeated in anguish.

'You don't have one?' Cameron held up a reassuring hand. 'Maybe that's something I can help you with.'

At that moment, the band on stage kicked into a raucous rockabilly stomp.

Cameron's brow creased in discomfort. 'Perhaps we could discuss this somewhere quieter?'

He held out his hand and, as if she'd been hypnotised, Natty put her hand in his.

6

Cameron led Natty upstairs with Matt hard on her heels and Margie, Jude and Jase chasing along behind. In the comparative quiet of the pub above, Cameron raised a thick black eyebrow at the extended group and slid an alligator wallet from inside his drape jacket.

'May I buy you all a drink?' he offered in his smooth, Scottish brogue.

'No, let me get it,' Matt cut in, possessively. 'What are you having, Natty?'

'Just cola!' She found the unexpected note of jealousy in Matt's voice rather thrilling, as if he were staking a claim on her. *As well he might!* Natty thought mischievously. The dark and brooding Cameron Swoon had a definite magnetism about him and he was devilishly handsome, too!

'A wise choice of drink,' said the ever-unsmiling Cameron. 'You need a clear head in the music business.'

'Is it coke for you, too, then?' Matt asked Cameron.

'Whisky, thank you,' Cameron returned dryly. 'A single malt, with no ice.'

He led Natty to a table in a corner alcove and the others crowded around.

Sitting back in his sharply-cut Edwardian suit, Cameron put a pair of neatly manicured hands palm down on the table.

'The first thing you have to understand, Natty, is that it's no' like it was in the Fifties when you could make a demo tape with just voice and guitar. Gary Morris is twenty-six. When a producer of his generation hears a demo, he wants it to sound like a finished record. Then he adds the sprinkling of stardust that turns it into a hit. So if we're going to do this, we'll have to do it properly. Have you given much thought to arrangements, Natty — the sort of instruments you'd like on your records?'

141

'I've got a few ideas,' Natty said, keenly.

'Good, because I have a friend who has a small studio on the other side of town. It's not cheap, but he owes me a favour. If we go for an evening slot it shouldn't cost too much. You're probably looking at five hundred, including the mix.'

'Five hundred pounds!' Natty gulped. Her credit card was maxed and she wasn't due a pay cheque until the end of the month. She hadn't even paid her rent yet.

To her surprise, Margie cut in with, 'I'm sure we can sort something out, Natty. This could be your big break!'

'That's very true,' Cameron confirmed. As Matt brought over a tray of drinks, Cameron went on, 'We'll need some top quality musicians, but hopefully we can find some who are prepared to work for promises.'

'How do you mean?' asked Margie.

Cameron glanced at the landlady, recognising the astute businesswoman behind the flamboyant exterior.

'Ninety percent of the music business is speculative,' Cameron explained. 'It's about getting in at the beginning of something and hoping it grows into something big. At the moment there's nae money in this for any of us. But if Gary gives Natty a record deal, she'll need a band. There will be national tours, TV, Europe, America. For the players who were in at the beginning, that's three or four years of full-time employment from a couple of top ten hits.'

Cameron turned his storm-cloud eyes to Natty and the corner of his mouth flickered into the smallest of smiles. 'And if we're talking about Gary Morris, I think we're talking top ten hits.'

'What's your cut in this?' Matt asked suspiciously.

Cameron gave Matt a hard stare, as if appraising him. Matt's cheeks began to colour, but he held the newcomer's eyes.

At length, Cameron said, 'At the moment, Matthew? Nothing. I'm no' asking Natty to pay me anything and I'm no' asking her to sign anything. If nothing comes of this, then Natty has paid for a professional quality demo and I've invested nothing but my time. At that point we can either take it around some other record companies or we can shake hands and you can carry on without me. That will be your choice.'

Cameron leaned forward and lowered his voice still further. His stormy eyes smouldered with intensity. 'But if this comes off and Gary offers Natty a record deal, she'll need a manager — and a good one. Hopefully, if it gets to that stage, I'll have had time to convince you that I'm the man for the job.'

The opening bars of Roy Orbison's *Only The Lonely* issued across the table from Cameron's jacket pocket. He slipped out a slim modern phone curiously at odds with his Fifties Teddy

Boy suit and nodded his slickly oiled quiff at Natty. 'If you'll excuse me, Natty, I need to take this call.'

As Cameron walked away from the table, Margie squeezed Natty's arm excitedly. 'Natty, you're going to be a star!'

'Only if Garry Morris likes my song, though!' Natty warbled. 'Whoever he is!'

'And only if we trust Mr Swoony-smoothy over there,' said Matt, in a tone that suggested he didn't trust Cameron one bit.

Jude stroked a teasing hand over Matt's flat top. 'You're just jealous that someone looks even more like Elvis than you do!'

Margie craned her neck to look at Cameron, where he was talking on his phone, near the bar.

'He's a cagey customer,' Margie agreed. 'But that's not a bad thing in business. My Alf was exactly the same. That's where you go wrong, Matt — you're always too open.'

'Thanks for your support, Mum!' retorted Matt, put out.

'Do you think we can trust him?' Natty asked Margie, worriedly. Her judgement where smooth, dark, handsome men were concerned hadn't been too good lately, but she trusted Matt's mum as much as anyone.

'I don't know, sweetie,' Margie admitted, thoughtfully. 'But if we don't sign anything and don't pay him anything, what have we got to lose?'

Matt turned to Jase who, as a part-time DJ, was the only one of them who knew anything about modern music. 'Have you heard of this Gary Morris?'

'I read an article about how he's some kind of reclusive genius,' said Jase. 'He spent a year developing three unknowns into 3-Dom and made them the biggest group on the planet. If Cameron can get your demo to him, Natty, you've got it made!'

Natty remembered all the billboards and newspaper photos of the three grinning girls that comprised 3-Dom.

Their images were everywhere. She imagined herself blowing a Marilyn Monroe-style kiss from the same pictures in their place. After the reception she'd had on stage, it didn't seem like such a remote prospect. Natty had always felt like a star on the verge of discovery. Perhaps her day was finally about to come!

As Jase spoke, Cameron returned to the table. He shot his cuffs, which were studded with cufflinks shaped like miniature playing cards, the six of hearts on his left wrist and the three of diamonds on his right. He laced his fingers in front of the watch chain that stretched across his smart pinstripe waistcoat.

'Well, Natty?' the Scot asked quietly. 'Do you think we can work together on this?'

Realising that she'd been doing a lot of improbable things lately, and that they'd all turned out better than she'd expected, Natty said dizzily, 'We can only give it a whirl!'

'This deserves a celebration!' Margie declared. Standing, she straightened her fringed leather skirt and gave Cameron the saucy look that thirty years ago had sold a million Coconut Crunch biscuits. 'Tell me, Mr Swoon, do you jive as well as that suit suggests you do?'

Cameron raised an eyebrow and paled, like an exceptionally well dressed rabbit caught in a set of headlights. 'Well . . .'

'Because I feel like a boogie!' With the thump of rock'n'roll pulsating through the floor from the club downstairs, Margie grabbed Cameron's hand and dragged him towards the door.

Sensing that Matt had been feeling sidelined since Cameron's arrival, Natty dragged her chair closer to him and cupped her hand around his muscular forearm.

'What about you?' Natty asked him. 'Do you dance?'

'Why? Are you asking?' Matt grinned down at her.

'Of course not,' Natty said primly. 'A

lady always waits for the gentleman to ask.'

Matt took her hand and his touch sent electric shocks through her.

'Well, in that case Miss Smalls, may I have the pleasure of this dance?'

'The pleasure will be all mine!'

As they leapt to their feet, Matt turned so quickly towards the door that he knocked over his chair and almost fell over it. Natty hugged him around the waist to save him from falling. The feel of his hard stomach muscles within her arms was as delicious as it was unexpected.

'I think I'm going to have to watch my feet on the dance floor!' Natty laughed as Matt recovered his balance. Giggling like teenagers, they ran to the door.

Watching them go, Jude pushed back her mass of chocolate brown curls and sighed. 'Young love, eh?'

Jase gazed speculatively at his housemate. 'Do you think we should go and show them how to bust some moves on the dance floor?'

'I'd be more likely to bust my knee,' observed Jude. 'But if you're buying, I could murder a drink.'

*   *   *

Downstairs, The Cinderella Club was really rocking. Duke and the Bop Tones were leaning forward over the edge of the stage in their tartan drape jackets as they charged through an ear-splitting version of Elvis's *Big Hunk Of Love*. The singer sounded just like the King himself. The slapping rhythm of the double bass and the thump of the bass drum sent a pulse through Natty's ribs and the twang of the guitar shot through her nerves like a lightning bolt.

Some of the tables had been pulled to the edges of the club and several couples were jiving in the middle of the room. Margie pulled Cameron into the thick of the swirling motion. With what little light there was illuminating her blonde bouffant, white biker jacket and fringed skirt, Margie spun and twirled around on the end of his wrist, doing all the work while the sombre-suited Cameron moved as little as possible.

'Let's show them how it's done!' Natty tugged Matt's hand.

Natty loved dancing, although in her experience most men weren't very good at it. Given Matt's clumsiness when he was excited, she didn't expect much from him in the way of fancy footwork and didn't mind. She was wearing heels for the stage, not pumps for jiving, so she'd be satisfied with a gentle pace and some simple moves. Just being on the floor with Matt and holding his hand would be thrilling enough.

Natty quickly discovered, however, that Matt was a far better jiver than she was. His crepe-soled shoes moved with perfect rhythm and he placed them with effortless precision. His big muscular body shimmied elegantly. He threw in fancy flourishes with his hands like one of the pros on *Strictly Come Dancing*. Halfway through the first song, Natty could tell Matt was using only a fraction of the skill he possessed: He was generously keeping things simple to make her look good.

'You're really good at this!' Natty shouted over the music; as her petticoats swirled up around her garters.

'Jen and I danced competitively!' Matt grinned. 'We were regional champions. All the acrobatic stuff.'

'This must seem tame to you!' remarked Natty, as she twirled under his arm.

'We can try some acrobatics if you like!' Matt grinned encouragingly.

'Not in these shoes!' Natty replied. She was already struggling to keep up. Ending up on her back would not be a good look!

As their third dance came to an end, Natty fell breathlessly against Matt's chest in a loose hug.

Partly she was tired — it had been an eventful evening. Mostly she just wanted the excuse to hug him in circumstances where it wouldn't be misconstrued as anything other than a friendly embrace between friends, even though it most certainly was!

Matt squeezed her to him. He stroked her hair where it was sleekly Kirby-clipped to the side of her head.

'Would you like to stop for a drink?' he asked her.

'No, but I'd love some air!'

They ran out onto the pavement and Natty sucked in a lungful of fresh sea breeze. After the intense heat of the club, and their exertions on the dance floor, the evening air felt icy cold. Its kiss on her heated skin was as exhilarating as a cold shower after a scalding bath.

Screaming with delight, Natty ran across the busy promenade to the opposite pavement. She vaulted onto the wrought iron handrail overlooking the beach and sat side-saddle, with her feet on the middle rail and her skirt and petticoats billowing around her stockings. She felt like a model in a 1950s poster for rail journeys to the coast.

Her heart still thumping, Natty gazed along the shop fronts of the prom. Light and noise spilled from amusement arcades, restaurants, fish and chip shops and bars. The evening had grown dusky and the signs were lit up like Las Vegas in swathes of pink, white and golden lights. With more illuminations strung from the street lamps and the headlights of cars ploughing up and down, the scene was every bit as magical as the lights of London's West End.

Natty wondered why she'd never noticed the beauty of her home town before. Why had she always believed the lights of Piccadilly Circus would be so much brighter?

Matt leaned on the rail beside her. The ever-changing lights of the prom dyed red and blue the close-cropped hair on the back of his head and brush-like flat top.

Natty followed his gaze out to sea. The tide was out, the moon was high and a wiggly line of white waves broke gently in the distant shadows of the beach. A bar of pink sunset still defined the horizon.

'What a night!' Natty enthused. 'I'm so glad you persuaded me to come!'

Matt smiled at her, rather wistfully, Natty thought, and said, 'Looks like it could be the beginning of a whole new career.'

'I hope so! Natty Smalls — singing sensation!' That was even better than Natty Smalls — ace reporter! 'Do you really think Cameron will be able to get my song to that producer?'

'I hope so,' said Matt. 'I asked Justin if he knew anything about this Cameron Whatisname. It seems he's been hanging around the local clubs for the past couple of weeks and said he was a talent scout for a couple of record companies. He sounds like he knows what he's talking about. At least you know that people like your song. I've never seen anyone get such a good reception on their debut.'

Natty relived the memory and hugged herself, excitedly. 'Oh, Matt, you don't know how it felt when they all started cheering! A girl could get used to it!'

'You certainly looked the part!' Matt grinned. 'It was as if you'd been singing all your life.'

Natty giggled. 'You should have seen your face when I sang that line to you!'

'Did you mean it?' he asked, teasingly.

'Don't ask, don't tell!'

Sliding off the handrail in a flurry of petticoats, she skipped and twirled on the pavement, still high on the adrenalin of everything that had happened.

Matt watched her admiringly.

'Fancy a walk on the beach?' he asked.

'Why not!' Natty enthused. To do anything else on such a perfect night would be a waste.

A flight of stone steps led down to the sand. As she followed Matt down, Natty remembered her shoes. In the shadows at the foot of the steps, she grabbed Matt's belt and turned him away from her.

'No peeking!' she admonished. Behind

his back, she hitched up her skirt and petticoats and rolled down her stockings. She popped them into her shoes and, picking them up in one hand, slipped her free hand into Matt's. 'Ready now.'

The sharp and gritty feel of the sand between her toes was exquisite — and so was the loose, warm feel of Matt's fingers around hers. The darkness was gathering around them and it lent a thrilling intimacy to the contact. As the lights and sounds of the prom receded it felt as if they were alone in the cool night.

They walked in silence towards the sea and Natty was grateful of the chance to relax and calmly absorb all the amazing things that had happened to her that evening. She felt safe with Matt. He wasn't the kind to make a grab for her. He was a nice guy through and through.

The stars were out, bringing a cosy half-light to the pale beach. The moon painted silvery highlights on the glassy sea. Standing on the wet sand near the water's edge, with the filmy extremity of the waves skimming gently towards her toes, then receding with a gossipy whisper, Natty held Matt's hand and doubted if she'd ever be part of a more romantic scene.

She wondered if he would kiss her. Remembering the far-too-brief taste of his soft, full lips in The Cinderella Club, she wondered what a proper, lingering smooch would be like out here beneath the moon and beside the softly lapping sea. She imagined he'd begin tentatively, his lips barely daring to brush hers. His shyness was one of the things Natty found most attractive about him. But then, encouraged, his lips would become bolder and more passionate . . .

Natty found herself becoming aroused at the thought. She ached to turn the fantasy into reality, but she was determined not to make the first move. In Natty's book that always had to come from the man!

At length, Matt said, 'I'm sorry I was

a bit off with Cameron earlier. I suppose I thought . . . well I thought he was looking at you like he fancied you.'

'Can't blame him for that!' Natty chirped in her distinctive sing-song voice.

Matt chuckled. 'No, I can't blame him for that.'

The word 'I' in that sentence, and the wistfulness of Matt's tone made Natty look up. Matt's eyes were in shadow, but she was taken aback by the intensity with which he was gazing at her. His fingers closed a little more firmly on hers and his thumb began to stroke the back of her hand. She felt her mouth go dry and heard her heart thumping in her chest.

'I know we haven't known each other long, Natty,' Matt said awkwardly. 'But I wondered if you'd like to go out with me.'

'We are out, aren't we?' Natty replied a little nervously.

Matt cupped her hand in both of his. His touch was as gentle as if he were cradling a wounded bird.

'I mean go out properly.' Matt grinned. 'To dinner, maybe?'

Natty caught her breath. Five minutes ago she'd been savouring the fantasy of a romantic clinch beside the waves. She imagined it like a scene in a movie. She could almost see it on the big screen with the surging romantic music stirring cinema goers to joyous tears as the camera panned away into a long shot of the star-crossed couple.

Dragged back to reality, Natty suddenly realised a kiss wouldn't be the final shot in a movie, it would be the beginning of something far more real. Again, she thought of all the responsibilities that went with dating a man like Matt.

Her mouth dry, Natty licked her lips nervously. Matt's big, chiselled, handsome face looked suddenly scared as if he were a barely teenage boy asking out a girl for the very first time. She couldn't bear to hurt him. But . . .

'You're married,' she whispered.

Matt smiled nervously. 'It's over

between me and Jen. You know that.'

Natty desperately wanted to believe him. But that wasn't the only issue. There was also Rosie. Natty wondered if she really wanted to be a stepmother, or if she were capable of being one. And could Matt possibly be looking for anything less than that from a woman at this point in his life?

Natty didn't want to rule it out — Rosie was so sweet. But a date with Matt suddenly felt like more than dinner. It felt as if she were committing to a lifetime, and she hadn't had enough time to think about that.

Hesitantly, Natty said, 'Do you think it's . . . a bit soon? With what's happening with Jen, I mean.'

Matt dropped her hand. He clenched his teeth and turned away in embarrassment.

'I'm sorry, Natty. I'm so clumsy sometimes. I thought you liked me, but I must have read it wrong. I'm sorry if I've embarrassed you.'

Natty was mortified. Matt took a few

steps away from her and it felt as if he was pulling something out of her heart.

'Of course I like you!' Natty blurted. 'It's not that . . . '

'You don't have to explain . . . '

Natty ran after him and grabbed his arm. 'Of course I'll go out with you!'

Matt turned, apprehensively. 'You're not just saying that because you feel sorry for me?'

Natty laughed and did the only thing she could think of. In fact, she didn't think of it, she did it before she realised she'd done it. She threw her arms around him, propped her chin on his chest and squeezed him tightly.

'Convinced?' Natty grinned, giddily.

Matt laughed with relief. 'More than!' he confirmed.

He put his hands on her shoulders and they felt like hot irons burning through her blouse. The heat spread through her as if she were on fire. Natty had never felt so physically attracted to a man.

He leaned forward to kiss her. She

stepped back, suddenly scared by the impulsiveness with which she'd embraced him, and afraid of what else she might do in the heat of the moment and regret later.

'What's wrong?' Matt asked.

Natty took a deep draught of the cool and salty air and let it out in a long sigh as she remembered the last time her impulsiveness had landed her in trouble.

'That fiancé I may have mentioned,' Natty began in an embarrassed tone. 'Lamborghini, Mayfair flat, a chain of fancy restaurants . . . '

'You're making me feel inadequate.' Matt grinned.

'He said he loved me, bought the ring, went down on one knee. Turned out he has another house in the country — and another woman and three kids I didn't even know about.'

'That's terrible!' Matt exclaimed.

'I guess it's left me a little . . . wary!' Natty sang the word with her trade-mark trill. She grinned to make light of it. But the truth was, 'wary' didn't cover how she felt. She was terrified of making another blunder.

'I'm not surprised you're wary! But you know it's not like that with me, don't you? It really is over between me and Jen.'

'No secret families hidden away?' Natty joked, nervously.

'Only Rosie,' said Matt, 'but you know about her.'

'I know, and she's lovely,' said Natty. 'I just wanted you to understand why I didn't jump at your invitation.'

'Thanks for telling me,' Matt said with relief. 'I thought I had BO or something!'

The sound of Elvis singing *All Shook Up* suddenly burst exuberantly from Matt's pocket.

'Is that a phone in your pocket,' Natty giggled, 'or are you just trying to tell me something?'

Matt pulled out his phone and checked the display. He looked a little embarrassed.

'It's Jen,' he said awkwardly. 'I'd

better answer in case it's about Rosie.'

'Of course.' Natty turned away to give him some privacy, and so he wouldn't see her deflated expression. Was this a forewarning of what a date with Matt would be like, Natty wondered? In fact, was that what life with Matt would be like — her, Matt, Rosie . . . and Jen?

'Hi babe,' Matt said brightly.

The 'babe' went into Natty's side like a knife. She guessed he used the endearment out of habit. He sounded nervous and the brightness in his tone was obviously false. She could hear the pain behind the cheeriness. She felt sorry for him, having an ex to whom he would always be linked, no matter what, because they shared a daughter.

Natty took a few steps away. Matt did the same in the opposite direction, and spoke into the phone with quiet irritation.

'I can't talk about that at the moment. I'm in The Cinderella Club with Mum and Jase. I know it sounds quiet, I've popped outside for a moment. No, I'm not with anyone else . . . '

Natty turned and gave him a sharp look, although his back was turned and he didn't see her. If it was all over between him and Jen, why couldn't he say he was with someone else?

Natty could hear the high, tinny sound of Jen's voice coming through the phone. She sounded angry. Natty guessed Matt was just trying to keep the peace.

Natty hugged herself, her shoes in her hand. Having felt so hot moments before, the breeze coming in from the sea was starting to feel chilly. The wet sand, which had felt so blissfully cool beneath her feet, felt cold and squidgy, like mud, between her toes now.

'I'll call you tomorrow.' Matt spoke without enthusiasm and pocketed his phone. He turned and gave Natty an apologetic little shrug.

'She just phoned up to have a go at me. Can't blame her, really. I shouldn't have answered.'

'Could have been about Rosie,' Natty said sympathetically.

'Could have been,' Matt agreed.

Natty gazed at him, sadly. His hair and T-shirt were white and ghostlike in the moonlight, his face shadowed. They'd drifted about ten feet apart on the darkened beach and the distance seemed symbolic. A few minutes ago she'd been holding his hand and fantasising about a cinematic romantic clinch. Then he'd actually been in her arms, her body burning for him so hotly she'd been scared she wouldn't be able to control herself.

In the space of a phone call, all that had disappeared. Natty mourned the loss of their brief intimacy as keenly as a bereavement, but there seemed no way to bring it back. Not tonight, anyway.

'We'd better get back to the club.' Matt smiled awkwardly. 'Mum and the others will be wondering where we are.'

He started to walk towards the distant lights of the prom. Natty followed him. Then, for the second time that evening, her body did something before her mind caught on. Her feet suddenly kicking up dry sand instead of mud, she took two long, quick strides to catch up with Matt. She grabbed his hand and fell into step with him.

He looked down at her in surprise, then grinned with relief.

'So where are you taking me for dinner?'

'Er . . . how about the Aquarium?' he replied.

'Ooooh, posh!'

'No more than you deserve!'

'I wasn't arguing!' Natty squealed with delight.

At the foot of the steps, Natty put down her shoes and looked at her feet in horror. Her skin pale in the moonlight, her feet were speckled with dry sand and streaked with dirty black mud. She couldn't put them in her shoes like that.

'Hold on a moment.' Natty searched her handbag for a wet wipe or a tissue, but she'd used her supply repairing her makeup earlier. 'Have you got anything I can wipe my feet on?'

'Allow me.'

Natty gasped as Matt pulled his T-shirt over his head. He had a chest like Mr Universe and a six-pack to go with it. Natty had never seen such a perfect torso. It was all she could do not to touch it to see if it was real.

While her mind was boggling at his physique, Matt dropped to his knees at her feet.

'You can't use your top!' Natty protested.

'It's going in the wash anyway.'

His touch light on her ankle, Matt lifted her right foot into his lap and began wiping it with the soft cotton. Natty marvelled at his gallantry . . . and at the way the unexpected massage was doing things inside her that had never been done before!

Natty gasped, as Matt's fingers explored the coastline of her instep. As he parted her smallest toes and rubbed the bunched cotton between them she let out a rising murmur.

'You're not ticklish, are you?' Matt grinned up at her. His face full of mischief in the moonlight, he began tickling her sole in earnest.

Natty shrieked loud enough to turn heads on the distant pier.

'Stop it!' she sang in a rising soprano. 'Stop it, STOP it!'

'Sorry!' Matt laughed. 'Couldn't resist it. Here, let me put your shoe on.'

'I feel like Cinderella!' Natty quipped, as she fanned her neck and tried to get her breath back.

'I don't think you're going to the ball, Cinders,' said Matt, as he waggled her foot and shoe. 'It won't go on.'

Investigating the blockage, Matt poked his fingers into the toe of the shoe. He pulled out her balled stocking and held it up, dangling full length between finger and thumb.

'Shall I put this on for you, too?' he said, hopefully.

Natty snatched the stocking and

thrust it into her bag.

'Just the shoe will be fine!' she sang deliriously.

'All right . . . there.' Matt eased the shoe onto her heel and set it down on the step. 'I'll just wipe your other foot.'

'No tickling . . . ' Natty began. She screamed shrilly enough to crack glass as Matt tickled her mercilessly.

Laughing, gasping and screaming, Natty lost her balance. She sat down heavily and sprawled backwards on the sandy stairs. As she did so, she saw four silhouetted figures leaning over the promenade handrail above her.

'Oh, er . . . hi, guys!' Natty sang.

Matt, stripped to his waist and holding Natty's bare leg, looked up to see his mum, Jase, Jude and Cameron looking down on them with amusement.

'Well!' Margie said in a saucy tone. 'I see you two are getting along well!'

7

The next day was Saturday and Natty was glad. Matt had to go and open the ice-cream parlour. Margie had to open her knicker shop. Jase had to go to the menswear store where he worked when he wasn't DJ-ing. And Natty could laze in the bath for as long as she pleased.

On a shelf in front of a steamed-up circular mirror, Natty propped her little pink portable CD player in the shape of a 1960s transistor radio and clicked on a compilation of soothing rock'n'roll ballads.

Her ruby red hair in a net, Natty propped her head on a pink polka-dot plastic cushion and slid deeply into the hot water beneath a mountain range of white rose-scented bubbles. With the foam tickling her chin, she closed her eyes and sang along to the Dixie Cups song about going to the chapel.

Natty was enjoying working at the newspaper. Mr Granger, the editor, was a sweet old man and he seemed to have taken her under his wing, which was useful as she was the only other member of staff. Natty was keen to learn, and the elderly newsman was happy to pass on his old-school newsgathering methods. His suits were as old as Natty's dresses — although he'd bought his new — and she thought they made a good team. Sitting behind the reception desk in the 1950s-style lobby, it was easy to imagine she was in classic 1930s newspaper flick *The Front Page*, even if the biggest story of the week concerned a proposal for a new supermarket.

But rushing her morning routine to get to the office meant Natty had some serious 'me' time to catch up on. Breathing slowly and deeply and letting her wrists and ankles float weightlessly in the soothing water, Natty decided her new career as a pop star would be a much more relaxing lifestyle — all day to pamper herself, do her make-up, fix her hair and choose her clothes before going on stage for an hour's work each evening.

There would be travel, of course, to LA, New York and Las Vegas. But Natty Smalls, world famous singing sensation, would have a private jet, probably with a marble bath on board so she could soak while she flew. A pink stretch limo would collect her from the sun-drenched airport and whisk her to Madison Square Garden. As she stepped onto the red carpet in a snow-white fur, she'd hear the adoring cheers and applause coming from inside the arena . . . cheers like the ones that had washed over her like a tidal wave at The Cinderella Club last night, only louder, much, much louder — a tsunami of adulation sweeping over the stage!

Natty stretched and purred at the thought. In the words of the Eddie Cochran song, that would be *Something Else*!

In the meantime, Natty had all day to pamper herself, do her make-up, fix her hair and choose her clothes before her evening dinner date with Matt. At the Aquarium, the poshest restaurant in town, no less!

As Elvis sang on the CD player, Natty relived her time with Matt on the beach. The touch of his fingers on her feet had been so electrifying that even the memory gave her the shivers.

With the evening suddenly seeming far too far away, Natty decided she'd pop into the ice-cream parlour to see him during the afternoon. It wasn't that she was chasing him; in Natty's book, that was definitely for the man to do. But it wouldn't hurt either of them to see each other earlier than planned, as a little taster of what was in store!

But what was in store? Natty wondered, in sudden despondency. With a sigh, she remembered Matt's phone call from Jen and how it had destroyed their romantic moment. How disappointing would it be if he took a similar call during a romantic dinner that was supposed to be for two? Or, worse, while they were enjoying a good-night smooch afterwards?

Would Matt take the call in such circumstances? Natty wondered. She wouldn't be able to complain if he did. As he'd said, last night, it might be about Rosie. Matt doted on his daughter, and Natty loved him for it. But she did wish his life wasn't so complicated.

★　★　★

Once she'd done her face and hair, and given herself a couple of squirts of Chanel No9, Natty put on a 1950s sundress in lime green and white diamond check. Sleeveless, with a square neck and wide buttoned shoulder straps, it had a pinched waist and cone-shaped skirt that flared to a wide hem just below her knee. She teamed it with stockings the colour of milky tea (Natty believed a lady should only ever go bare-legged on the beach) adding white stilettos with a pointed toe, and her late grandmother's silver watch.

It was noon, Natty noted with satisfaction, a civilised hour for a lady to greet the day.

As Natty reached the foot of the stairs, there was a smart rap on the door knocker. She opened the door to find Cameron Swoon on the step, sun gleaming off black hair oiled into a quiff the size of a crash helmet.

'Good afternoon, Natty,' the Scotsman said with the faintest flicker of a smile in one corner of his lips. 'I'm glad to see you don't only dress in style at night.'

'Likewise,' Natty observed, giving him a swift appraisal. Cameron was wearing a beautifully tailored medium grey suit with a fingertip-length drape jacket over a maroon Paisley pattern waistcoat. His black ribbon tie was tied in a neat bow and on his feet, Natty noted with approval, was a pair of highly polished, stout black brogues.

Only a man truly au fait with Edwardian fashion would have chosen such stylish footwear instead of the crepe soles or winkle-pickers which most people considered the only Teddy Boy shoes.

'Appearances are very important in this business, as you ken yourself,' said Cameron. 'The moment you stepped on stage last night you looked like a star. You'd won them over before you sang a word.'

'Flattery will get you everywhere! Well, it will get you a cup of tea, anyway! Would you like to come in?'

'That's very kind of you.'

'Close the door behind you, then!' Conscious of Cameron's admiring gaze on her pert girdle-shaped rear — and not minding, because what else was an hour-glass figure for if not to be admired? — Natty led the Scot down the hall to the kitchen.

'Take a seat!' Natty waved him to a stool at the breakfast bar and skipped over to the kettle.

'I dropped by to say I've made some phone calls,' said Cameron. 'I've booked the recording studio for Wednesday evening. Duke and the Bop Tones from the club last night are going to play on the session.'

'Wow!' said Natty. 'They're really good.'

'The rockabilly stuff is just what they do for a bit of fun,' Cameron revealed. 'They're all professional studio musicians by day, so I'm expecting good results. I've also booked a photo shoot for Tuesday.'

'Photos?' Natty turned on her heel.

'You're a beautiful lassie with a unique sense of style. We need some pictures to go with the music.' Cameron put his head on one side and gave her an appraising look. 'I was thinking of something moody, black and white and soft focus, like one of those old Hollywood glamour shots from the Forties. I can just see you in an off-the-shoulder mink.'

Natty gazed into space. She pictured herself on the cover of Fifties movie mag *Photoplay* wearing nothing but a seductive simper and a strategically draped fur stole.

'Sounds like we're singing from the same hymn book!' she replied. Then she noticed the dreaminess in Cameron's eyes as he studied her. She remembered Matt's comment about Cameron fancying her, and felt a blush rising to her throat. Glad to hear the kettle click off behind her, she skipped to the cupboard in search of some cups.

'Who's the artist?' Cameron asked, as Natty poured the tea.

Natty glanced over her shoulder and saw that Matt had left his sketchbook on the breakfast bar. Cameron had begun leafing through it.

'Oh, that's Matt's book,' Natty grinned. 'He's so talented, isn't he?'

'Very,' Cameron agreed.

Natty carried two cups to the breakfast bar and sat opposite the Scot.

'So, what are you doing this evening?' Cameron asked.

'Er?' Natty sat up, sharply.

'There's not long until the recording session,' Cameron went on, deadpan. 'I was hoping the band could come over tonight to rehearse some songs with you.'

'Oh!' Natty breathed a sigh of relief. She'd thought for a moment he was asking her out.

'You dinnae have anything already planned?' the Scot asked. 'Only this demo could be the biggest break you ever get, Natty. I think we should give it some priority.'

Natty was about to mention her date with Matt. But Cameron was right. She'd never been in a recording studio or worked with a band; she would certainly need all the rehearsal time she could get.

Besides, she reasoned, going forward into a relationship with Matt was still rather a scary proposition. She wouldn't feel too guilty about taking the opportunity to put it off for a while.

'Tonight would be perfect!'

'Good. Now, about that mink for the

photos. Do you have such a thing or shall we take a stroll into town and see if we can find something suitable?'

'A shopping trip?' Natty cried in delight. 'For mink? I think you'll find, Mr Swoon, that is something no girl has ever been known to turn down! Not this girl, at any rate!'

Secretly, Natty found the prospect of being squired to the shops by the immaculately tailored Cameron quite exciting.

She thought of poor Matt, slaving away behind the counter in the ice-cream parlour, but didn't feel too guilty. After all, her relationship with Cameron was purely business, wasn't it?

'Would you like a bite to eat before we go?' Natty asked.

'That would be very kind of you,' said Cameron smoothly.

* * *

'And then there were two!' chortled the newspaper seller on the corner, as

Natty strolled by with her white-gloved hand hooked in the elbow of the drape-suited Cameron. 'Having fun?'

'More than you could imagine!' Natty answered, giving him a flirty look over the top of her sunglasses.

'This time you *must* be going to a wedding!' the news-seller called after them.

'We'll see!' Natty warbled.

As they crossed the road at the lights, Natty saw their reflection in a shop window opposite. It was no wonder she and Cameron were attracting so many admiring glances from the Saturday afternoon shoppers. Even she had never seen such a well turned-out couple!

Snatching a sideways glance at their reflection in another window, Natty couldn't help noticing the resemblance between Cameron's long grey jacket and a wedding suit. With his solemn expression, he looked as though he were walking her along the aisle to give her away. Natty wondered if it was an omen. She wondered idly if Matt owned an Edwardian drape suit, or whether Cameron could recommend a good tailor. She certainly couldn't marry Matt in his T-shirt and biker jacket! Not when she had her vintage bridal gown worked out to the last detail.

Natty had been back in town long enough to know where to start hunting mink but, before they headed to that end of town, she tugged Cameron's arm towards Matt's ice-cream parlour.

'Shall we get a coffee?' she asked. She had to tell Matt about the change to their plans for later. She also wanted to see his handsome, grinning face. It felt like days since their walk on the beach the previous evening.

As they waited for a gap in the taxis and tourist buses, Cameron cast an admiring eye over the ice-cream parlour.

'Looks like the laddie's doing all right for himself,' he said with a nod towards the shop.

Natty swelled with pride on Matt's

behalf, then admitted, 'It's a pity his wife owns half of it. When they divorce he said he'll probably have to sell up.'

'Really?' Cameron noted the news with a raised eyebrow, his face otherwise showing no expression.

Natty wished Matt's wife didn't keep intruding into her thoughts. As they crossed the road, though, it wasn't Jen who put Natty suddenly on Amber Alert.

Through the glass door of the ice-cream parlour, Natty saw the unmistakable shape of Jude, with her huge frizz of chocolate curls and long, willowy body draped in a patterned, ankle-length hippy dress.

Jude was sitting on a high stool at the counter but leaning forward, with her elbows on the chrome worktop. Matt was mirroring her pose from the other side. Their faces were close and Matt was wearing a soulful expression, as if they were having a heart-to-heart.

The bell jangled as Natty burst in.

'Hi, you two — hope I'm not

interrupting anything!' Natty called, trying to keep her voice light.

Matt leapt to his feet. 'Hi Natty — no, of course not!'

Jude let out a little giggle and slipped from her stool with catlike grace.

'I was just leaving anyway,' she said, with a contented smile. 'Bye, Matt!'

Jude gave him a tinkly little wave and swept from the parlour with her usual airy nonchalance. Two women came in with baby buggies and, with a small queue forming, Natty realised it wasn't the moment for jealous questions.

'What can I get you?' Matt asked, red-faced.

'Two coffees, please, Matthew.' Cameron slipped out his alligator wallet.

Matt held up his palm. 'They're on the house! Take a seat, I'll bring them over.'

Natty and Cameron sat face to face on the high stools in the window. Natty crossed her legs, the knee of her tea-coloured stocking almost brushing the sharply pressed grey wool of

Cameron's trousers. With white-gloved fingers she adjusted the hem of her lime and white sundress to make sure her knee was shown off to its best advantage.

While Matt dealt with his other customers, Natty noticed him casting suspicious looks at her and the well-dressed Scottish Teddy Boy in the corner. Turning her lips into rosebuds, she made a show of checking her lipstick in the mirror of her makeup compact and relished the opportunity to make Matt wonder if he had any competition.

Matt looked gratifyingly jealous, but at the same time Natty felt suddenly anxious about cancelling her dinner date. Could she risk leaving Matt unoccupied with Jude on the prowl?

Natty found it hard to believe Matt would prefer Jude to her. But Jude was an attractive woman and one without scruples, Natty reckoned. Matt and Jude had probably known each other a long time and they were definitely close. Her mind racing, Natty wondered if they had had something going on together in the past. After all, there had to be a reason why his marriage had hit the rocks.

When Matt brought the coffees over, Natty explained about having to postpone dinner for the rehearsal. Matt's face fell like an avalanche.

Cameron said smoothly, 'You're welcome to come and watch, of course. I'm sure Natty would welcome your support.'

'Wouldn't miss it!' Matt grinned with relief.

'And in the meantime,' Natty said, smugly, 'Cameron's taking me shopping for a new coat!'

'It's for a photo shoot,' Cameron said quickly. 'It's very important that we give Gary Morris a music and pictures package. Actually, Matthew, I couldnae help noticing that you're a rather good artist. I was wondering if you might give some thought to an album cover design. Anything we can give Gary to show him how seriously Natty has been thinking about her career can only be helpful.'

'Hmmm.' Matt gave Cameron an appraising look. 'How did you come to know this producer, anyway?'

The corner of Cameron's lips flickered. Quietly, he said, 'There aren't many people in the music business I haven't met in the past ten years, Matthew. I was actually one of the first people to meet Gary, when he was putting 3-Dom together. I bumped into him in a club where he was checking out Kelly as a possible member of the group.

'Nobody had heard of Gary at that point; he was working completely on his own from a little studio he'd set up in his flat. He invited me round to play me some music he'd been working on and within a few minutes I knew I was in the presence of a creative genius.'

Cameron turned to engage Natty. 'Do ye ken the set-up with Gary? Like a lot of producers these days, Gary has his own production company. He makes the records and leases them to the record company.

'Now, at the time I met him, Gary didnae have any contacts. Without being unduly modest, I didnae exactly broker the deal between Gary and the record company, but I opened some doors for him, introduced him to the right people. Since then, he's always looked to me as a kind of advisor.'

Cameron looked Natty in the eye and said, 'That's why I'm confident he'll listen when I tell him you're the next big thing.'

8

'What do you think?' Natty twirled excitedly in the middle of Margie's all-white living room. She was wearing a bigger, fluffier and whiter fur coat than she had ever dreamed existed. The collar framed her face. The hem swished an inch above the floor and flared as widely a crinoline. The cuffs were big enough to hide a chihuahua in. Natty felt like a snow queen. Or a sexy snowball. Or a living meringue.

'Wow!' Matt uttered.

'Or you can wear it like this, as if I'm wearing nothing underneath!' Natty shrugged the collar down to her upper arms and blew Matt a kiss over her bare shoulder.

Matt's eyeballs bulged like ping-pong balls. 'Are you wearing anything underneath?' he asked, mesmerised.

'Aha — that's something you'll never

know!' Natty hiked the fur back up around her neck and snuggled into the collar. 'And that's because I'm never going to take it off — ever!'

'Oh, Natty, you look just like Marlene Dietrich!' Margie declared excitedly.

'I bet it looked good on its original owners, too.' Jude smiled, her chocolate curls bouncing behind her as she swept into the room in her long, faded hippy dress. 'Don't you feel guilty about all the poor little minks who gave their lives?'

Natty gave Jude a reproachful look. She still hadn't had a chance to find out what that little tête-à-tête between Jude and Matt had been all about.

'Well, I wouldn't buy a new one.' Natty stroked the sleeve of the coat with reverence. Her hand completely disappeared in the long fur. 'But these poor little fellows died in the 1940s. They're dead anyway, so not wearing it would be even worse than keeping their memory alive.'

'It must have cost a million!' Matt said in awe. He shot a jealous look in Cameron's direction, wondering if the expensively dressed Teddy Boy had picked up the tab.

'Oh, it wasn't so much,' said Natty. She hugged the coat to her body like a lover. 'I've only hired it until Wednesday. Although I might have to flee the country before then, so I don't have to take it back.'

She gave Matt a flirty smile. 'Fancy coming with me?'

'I'll start packing now!'

'I wouldnae flee the country too quickly,' Cameron said in his typically deadpan Scottish burr. 'If Gary Morris gives you a record deal, you'll be able to buy a coat like that for every day of the week.'

'And we'll all have to go through your agent just to speak to you!' Margie joked.

Natty struck a starry pose. 'Don't worry, Margie, I'll never forget my humble origins!'

'3-Dom got a million advance,' Cameron said, levelly.

'A million?' Natty squealed as if she'd touched a live wire. 'We'd better start rehearsing, then!'

Natty had wondered how Margie would take the news that her living room was to be turned into a rehearsal studio. She could imagine the consternation if she'd suggested rehearsing a rockabilly band in her parents' council house. As Duke and the Bop Tones carried their instrument cases, amplifiers and microphones up the hall, however, Margie was in her element. A house filled with music, art and creative people was her dream come true.

Watching the flamboyant landlady fuss around in her towering blonde bouffant and clingy white dress, handing out glasses of wine and plates of food while the band set up, Natty thought again what a fantastic mother-in-law Margie would make.

Natty jumped as the drummer crashed a cymbal like a gong. Duke, the guitarist and band leader leaned in to a retro chrome microphone set up on a stand in the middle of the living room. In an echoing Elvis voice, he drawled, 'Calling Miss Smalls to Studio B, we're, uh, ready to roll.'

Natty settled her guitar strap over the enormous cream puff of her coat.

'Are you really going to keep your coat on?' Matt grinned, as he perched on the sofa.

Natty gave him a look of wide-eyed innocence and said in her best Marilyn Monroe-style breathy whisper, 'I'm afraid I have to, with all these people around!'

While Natty was plugging her guitar in, Cameron said to the band, 'It's good of you gentlemen to do this unpaid.'

'Well, sir, we wouldn't normally,' Duke drawled into the microphone in his Elvis voice. 'But if you can get the tape to Gary Morris we'd, uh, be mighty pleased to be on it! So how does this first one go, Miss Smalls?'

Natty was showing the band the

chords to *Second Chance*, her plugged-in guitar ringing throughout the house, when Margie frowned. 'Was that the doorbell? I'd better go and check.'

Engrossed in her music, Natty barely noticed Margie leave the room. She was scarcely aware of the front door opening in the hall. Then, barely perceptibly through the ring of her guitar strings, a voice plucked at the edge of her attention. Her stomach tightened queasily before her mind fully registered the posh accent.

'Natty,' said Margie, coming back into the room, 'there's a gentleman caller . . . '

Natty looked up in horror as David Royale stepped out of her past and into the living room.

He was as devilishly suave and assured as they day they'd met. Natty's stomach flipped and her knees jellified exactly as they had then, although it was for totally different reasons now.

A youthful forty, with the tan of a man who flew regularly to Athens and Milan to source the ingredients for his restaurants, Royale looked as if he was auditioning for the role of James Bond. His black hair was rakishly slicked back. A black thousand-pound suit, the jacket unbuttoned, hung casually from his trimly athletic frame, over an open-necked shirt. In one hand he held two dozen dark red roses wrapped in silky paper.

Her throat suddenly too tight to speak, Natty began to shake. Despite what they said about fiery redheads, Natty had never liked confrontations. That's why she'd fled London without leaving a note.

Everyone in Royale's circle seemed slightly afraid of him, as if he wasn't a man to be crossed. Natty reckoned it had something to do with the way he hacked at the meat with his cleaver when he was doing his celebrity chef bit in the kitchen. She'd never seen him actually be violent but, as angry and betrayed by him as she'd felt, she'd decided not to risk physical injury on top of the emotional kind. She'd left her engagement ring on top of the evidence of Royale's double life and let him work out for himself why she'd gone.

After a few days with no sign of Royale, Natty had started to believe she'd never see him again — and especially not here. His apparent lack of contrition took her breath away.

Taking their lead from Natty's stunned silence, no one else in the room spoke.

Accustomed to being the centre of attention and the one in control of every situation, Royale gazed slowly around the room as if he owned it. He raised a sardonic eyebrow at the three musicians with their tartan jackets, double bass, drums and keyboard. He glanced at Cameron, who was watching silent and unsmiling from where he was perched on the arm of the sofa in his grey Edwardian suit. Then Royale's eyes fell on Matt, with his blonde flat top, white T-shirt and vintage jeans, who was looking up, rather worriedly, at him from the sagging sofa seat.

Unhurriedly, Royale's gaze returned

to Natty who was standing in front of a microphone in the centre of the room in her powder-puff mink, cradling her sunburst-orange Gretsch.

'Hello, Natty.' Royale's voice was as smooth and rich as slowly poured brandy. 'I see you're making good use of the guitar I bought you. You could do this in London, you know. I'd hire you some proper musicians.'

'How did you find me?' Natty hated the way her voice came out in a squeak. David was the one who was supposed to be feeling awkward, not her!

Royale shrugged. 'Once I tracked down your mother, she told me where you were staying. Of course, it would have been easier to get in touch if you came into the twenty-first century and bought a phone like everyone else.'

'I didn't want you to find me!' Natty blurted. She started to breathe quickly as her upset turned to anger and her anger turned to strength.

'I've been worried about you,' returned Royale.

'You've got your other woman to keep you company!' Natty retorted. 'And your three kids!'

Royale smiled and rolled his tongue around the inside of his cheek as if faintly embarrassed to be discussing some minor misunderstanding in public. 'Perhaps we could discuss this on the way back to London . . . ?'

'You really think I'm going back to London with you?' Natty stammered in disbelief.

Royale held out his hand in invitation. 'What was that line you were singing when I came in? '*Everyone deserves a second chance* . . . '?'

'Two houses and two girlfriends does *not* deserve a second chance!' Natty assured him.

From the arm of the sofa beside her, Cameron spoke quietly, but with an edge of steel in his Scottish burr. 'Do you wish to speak to this gentleman, Natty?'

'No,' Natty said in a trembling voice. With all her hurt suddenly bursting to the surface, she screamed at Royale, 'Get out! I never want to see you again!'

'Come now, Natty . . .' Royale took a step forward and Natty backed away.

Cameron stood up and put himself between Natty and the unwelcome guest.

'I think the lassie's made herself clear.' Cameron spoke with quiet menace. He spread his open palms and gave Royale a hard expectant look, like a publican shooing out stragglers at closing time.

'Yes, I think you'd better go.' Matt stood up beside Cameron, forming a wall.

A thrill ran through Natty at the sight of two big, handsome men protecting her. They were certainly a fine pair of specimens, she thought. Matt was a big man, with gym-sculpted muscles bulging out of his T-shirt. Cameron wasn't so big, but there was an unsmiling, self-contained quality about him that radiated an inner toughness.

Emboldened, Natty yanked the guitar

strap over her head. She loved the Gretsch guitar as much as anything she'd ever owned, but she suddenly didn't want to own anything with a connection to a man who had lied to her so cruelly. She held the instrument out in a shaking fist.

'Take this with you!' she shouted. 'It's probably what you came looking for.'

Royale looked unimpressed by either Natty's anger or the two men in front of him.

'Keep it,' he said calmly. 'And have the roses, too — something to remind you that I'll be there when you finally come to your senses.'

'I don't want your roses!' Natty shouted.

'I'll leave them with your friend, then.' Royale put the bunch of roses in Matt's arms. He looked Cameron up and down and said, quietly, 'That's a nice suit — do you think that style's coming back into fashion?'

'Out!' Cameron stepped forward, his face unmoving.

David turned to the door with a derisive snort. 'Okay, I'm going . . . but here's a parting gift for you, my Scottish friend.'

Without warning Royale spun back, his fist swinging at Cameron's face.

Cameron ducked with the speed of a boxer. The fist flew through the air and smacked into Matt's chin with the thwack of a cricket bat hitting a six. Matt went down like a house of cards.

'Matt!' shrieked Natty and Margie.

With typical economy of movement, Cameron seized Royale's arm and twisted it painfully behind his back. Holding the pinned arm with one hand and Royale's shirt collar with the other, Cameron drove the unwanted visitor out of the room, along the hall, through the front door and down the outside steps with the speed of an express train.

Behind them, Duke leaned into the microphone and said in his Elvis voice, 'And, uh-huh, the bad guy has left the building!'

Parked at the kerb was a sleek, low,

gun-metal grey Lamborghini. Cameron pinned Royale face down across the roof.

'I take it I dinnae have to spell oot what will happen if you ever bother Natty again?' Cameron said quietly.

His arm twisted too painfully to speak, Royale dumbly nodded his grudging agreement. Cameron let him go and pointed. 'London's that way. Dinnae come back.'

Royale, struggling to regain his composure, straightened his crumpled jacket and opened his car door.

'Don't expect to ever get a meal in one of my restaurants,' he muttered sourly, before gunning the Lambo's throaty engine and roaring away.

Back in the house, Natty, Margie and Jude were squatting anxiously around Matt who was sitting dazed on the floorboards.

'Are ye all right, laddie?' asked Cameron, who hadn't so much as creased his suit or put a hair out of place.

'He caught me with a lucky one!'

Matt grinned dizzily.

'Let me kiss it better,' said Natty. Gently, she tilted his head and planted a pink Cupid's bow lip print on the end of his square chin. 'Is that better?'

'Mmmm. Much better!'

'Does anywhere else hurt?' Natty asked, teasingly.

'Only my ego,' grinned Matt.

'Hmmmm,' Natty said thoughtfully. 'Let's see if this helps.'

Turning his face towards her, she pressed her lips softly and chastely to his.

'Well . . . Matt!' Margie said in an impressed tone. 'You are getting the best treatment.'

'You don't get that on the NHS,' Jude agreed, breezily.

Suppressing a giggle, Natty lifted her lips from Matt's. She did enjoy kissing him in front of Jude, though. It felt as though she were claiming him.

'Better?' Natty asked, with a raised eyebrow.

Matt waggled his hand in a 'maybe/

maybe not' gesture and said, 'I think I might need another dose.'

'We'll have to see how you're getting on tomorrow, then!' Playfully ruffling Matt's flat top, Natty stood up.

She turned to Cameron, who had been watching the ministrations with an unreadable expression. Briefly, Natty wondered if he should have been the one rewarded with a kiss. The efficiency with which he'd removed David Royale from the house was rather thrilling!

'Thanks for dealing with David,' Natty said shyly. 'I don't know how I ever got caught up with a rat like that.'

'Anyone can make a mistake,' Cameron said quietly. 'It's none of my business but if I were you, I'd stick to the nice guys like Matt in future. Shall we get on with the rehearsal?'

9

'Mmmmmm!' Natty snuggled beneath her duvet, luxuriating in the caress of the warm cotton on her skin and the inky blackness of the sleep mask that covered her eyes. Natty always enjoyed a lie-in on a Sunday . . . or indeed any other day!

A rap on the door made her jump. Matt's voice called, 'Are you awake, Natty?'

'I am now!' Natty sang back. The door was bolted, but she noticed he didn't try the handle. Matt was a perfect gentleman.

'Would you like to come out for Sunday lunch?' called Matt. 'Nice pub on the seafront?'

Natty sat up in her Fifties baby doll nightie, hairnet and eye-mask and did a quick mental calculation. 'Can you give me . . . an hour, Matt?'

On the other side of the door, he laughed. 'I guessed you'd say that. That's why I called you with over an hour to spare!'

'You know me so well!'

'I've run you a bath,' Matt called. 'Don't let it go cold.'

'Are you taking breakfast orders?' Natty called cheekily.

'If you like.' Matt chuckled.

'One boiled egg and soldiers, please!'

'And would madam like her back scrubbed, too?' Matt called, hopefully.

'Madam will manage on her own, thank you!'

As Natty rushed excitedly through her morning routine, she thought through her clothing options. Sunday lunch on the seafront meant a stroll on the beach afterwards, she reckoned, so something casual and practical was in order.

She opted for a pair of shiny satin trousers, high-waisted and elasticated at the ankles, with vertical navy and white stripes in a style she'd seen a young

Joan Collins wear on a vintage copy of *Picture Goer*. She teamed it with a similarly shimmering red satin blouse with elbow-length sleeves that was plain in every respect apart from the buttons, which were dinky white squares with tiny black dots on them, like dice.

Not wanting to be caught out on the beach in heels again, Natty laced her bare feet into pink and black canvas sneakers. It was a real Californian high school cheerleader look, she thought proudly, as she admired herself in the mirror. She stuffed a beach towel into a large rope shoulder bag.

As a final touch, Natty snipped the heads off half a dozen daffodils she'd bought in the high street the previous afternoon and kept in water overnight. She pinned three to each side of her head — two streaks of yellow through the swept-back red. Hooking her Twinco sunglasses in the neck of her blouse, Natty bounced excitedly down the stairs.

In the kitchen she found Jude, her

long willowy body shimmering in a silk kaftan in maroon with a gold pattern of camels, elephants and pyramids. Busy making tea, Jude swished her cascading chocolate curls over her shoulder and gave Natty a toothy grin before adding, 'I've put your roses in some water.'

Natty wrinkled her nose at the display on the breakfast bar. 'Do you really think I want a reminder of David Royale?'

'Roses are roses,' Jude answered airily. 'They're just as beautiful wherever they come from.'

'Hmmm.' Natty gave the dark red roses a second look and couldn't resist a sniff of their delicate scent. Jude was right, of course — Natty had already come to the same conclusion about her beloved Gretsch guitar. Last night she would have quite willingly given it back to David in order to close that chapter of her life. But if he truly didn't want it returned . . . did the instrument look any less beautiful or sound any less sweet than it ever had?

Also on the breakfast bar was a boiled egg in a china cup and a plate of golden brown toast, dripping with butter and neatly sliced into soldiers. Natty touched the egg with her palm and felt a fresh surge of love for Matt. The egg was warm; he'd timed it perfectly.

'Would you like tea?' Jude waggled a teapot.

'Thanks.' Natty sat on a stool at the breakfast bar and glanced over her shoulder. 'And while we're alone, I'd like a word with you.'

Jude raised an elegant eyebrow, questioningly. Natty envied the woman's cool composure. Her own heart was drumming and she almost chickened out of going on. But the question had to be asked.

'Is something going on between you and Matt?'

'Matt?' Jude looked caught off guard. Then her lean, tanned face composed itself into a picture of ecstasy. 'Mmmmm. We've been having a hot, torrid affair for months.'

'You have?' Natty felt as if her stool were falling through the floor beneath her.

'In my dreams!' Jude laughed. 'Of course there's nothing going on between me and Matt. I'm old enough to be his mother. Well, if I'd had him really young . . . '

'You looked pretty close in the ice-cream parlour yesterday,' Natty said with narrowed eyes.

'We are close,' Jude said airily. 'Close friends.'

'So what was the big heart-to-heart about?' Natty pressed.

Jude put her head on one side, as if considering whether to answer. Eventually, she said, lightly, 'That's Matt's business — you'll have to ask him.'

'But there's nothing going on between you?' Natty fretted.

'Of course there's not, and I'm glad you're getting on well with Matt.' Jude brought two cups over to the breakfast bar and sat opposite. 'It's a long time since I've seen him so happy.'

'Really?' Natty sliced the top off her egg and dipped a soldier into the warm yolk. It was a routine that always took her back to the simple, cosy days of childhood.

At length, Jude said, 'The one you should be watching is Jen. It's not the first time they've broken up, and you're not the first girlfriend he's had in the meantime. But they've always got back together again.'

Natty studied Jude's eyes, trying to work out whether she was being helpful or deliberately divisive. With Jude it was sometimes hard to tell.

With more confidence than she felt, Natty declared, 'Matt said they're really finished this time.'

'Maybe,' Jude said lightly. 'But never forget, Jen will always be the mother of his daughter. That's a powerful connection.'

The front door opened with a clatter and slammed shut. Matt came bopping up the hall in his crepe-soled black suede shoes.

'I've brought the car round to the front. Are you guys ready?'

'Guys?' Natty echoed in surprise. Wasn't this supposed to be lunch for two?

'Our carriage awaits!' Jude said, grinning. Slipping off her stool, the willowy woman hung a small glittery handbag over her slim shoulder by a long strap. She linked her free arm through Matt's and fell into step with him.

Struggling to catch up with the apparent change of plan, Natty dropped her empty plate in the sink and hurried into the hall after Matt and Jude. She was just in time to see Margie burst from the living room in a cloud of cigarette smoke and perfume, followed by the balding Jase who had a pair of iPod earplugs jammed in his ears and the tinny sound of dance music jingling around him.

'Are we all going?' Natty said trying to hide her surprise.

Matt blinked. 'Of course we are. We

always go to Sunday lunch together. That's why I wanted you to come with us!'

★ ★ ★

Matt parked the Chevy in the sun towards the end of the prom, outside a sprawling pub with a raised dining terrace at the front. The terrace was busy, but Matt had reserved a table by the wall, giving them a fabulous view across the prom to the glittering sea.

Natty sat next to Jase, with Matt, Margie and Jude opposite. While they waited for their food, Jude grinned across the table. 'So, Natty, what first attracted you to the handsome millionaire David Royale?'

Natty laughed and rolled her eyes. 'Oh, the usual attributes of handsome millionaires! The magic wand of a platinum credit card. Anything you want — ting! — it's there!'

Margie sighed nostalgically. 'It's wonderful when they do that, isn't it?

When my Alf was the biscuit king of England we had everything. Rolls Royce, boat, diamonds . . . '

'How come I never meet a man like that?' asked Jude.

'It's because you're too unmaterialistic,' Margie said, dismissively. 'Men sense you're not impressed by money, so they don't waste it on you.'

'I've never said I wouldn't be impressed by a boat or a Rolls Royce,' Jude protested. 'I've just never met anyone who could afford them.'

Matt grinned across the table to Jase. 'You see the only thing women want us for, Jase?'

'It's all mine wanted from me,' Jase agreed with a rueful look. 'Big house, big car . . . then when she had it all, she decided she could do without me!'

'Same thing with Jen,' Matt agreed, miserably.

'Oh, Matt.' Margie put a reassuring arm around her son. 'Of course we don't only want men for their money, do we, girls?'

Winking broadly at Natty, she added, 'It just helps if they've got a bit of money, too!'

'Oh, well. No chance for me, then,' Jase joked.

'Nor me,' said Matt. 'Not once Jen's finished with me. She's determined to get the house and the ice-cream parlour.'

'You'll bounce back,' Margie returned briskly. 'Just like your dad always did.'

Margie turned to Natty. 'We joke about men with money, but do you know when I felt most in love with my Alf? When the biscuit business went bust and we had to start again with absoluely nothing.'

'You don't think you'll patch things up with Jen, then?' Jase asked Matt.

The name tore at Natty's insides, the way a fingernail snags in nylon. *Why did Jen have to come into every conversation?* she wondered, bitterly.

Natty glanced worriedly at Matt, but when she saw he was gazing thoughtfully at her, she felt suddenly self-conscious and strangely guilty. Natty wanted Matt more than she'd ever wanted anyone. But she didn't want to be the reason he left his wife. She didn't want to feel like 'the other woman'.

Although Natty desperately wanted to give Matt an encouraging smile, she forced herself to look away. If Matt was going to leave Jen, she wanted it to be wholly his decision, the choice he would have made whether Natty was around or not.

As Natty gazed out to sea, she heard Matt sigh and say, 'Not this time, mate. We've tried in the past, for Rosie's sake, but there's only so long you can go on pretending. Living a lie's got to be worse for Rosie than being apart, hasn't it?'

Nobody answered. Natty guessed it was because nobody knew the answer. She certainly didn't.

It was strange, Natty reflected. Whenever she thought about a future with Matt on his own, she thought with total clarity: *yes, this is right*. But whenever she thought about Matt and Jen and Rosie, the family he was breaking up, she felt out of her depth.

Natty remembered the last time she'd seen Rosie, bawling her eyes out as Jen snatched her from Matt and stormed out of the ice-cream parlour. The thought of the poor child being torn between her mother and father made Natty so sad that she couldn't help feeling ending their marriage was wrong. She didn't know whether she had it within her to make the situation right.

An awkward silence was broken by the arrival of a waitress with their plates of steaming roast pork and chicken.

* * *

When lunch was over, Margie and Jude said they were going into town to go shopping. Jase headed for the Sunday market to look for old LPs.

'Fancy a walk along the beach, Natty?' Matt said casually.

'I thought you'd never ask!' Natty replied.

The beach was busy and they walked hand-in-hand away from the prom in search of a quieter stretch.

Natty eyed some children playing by the water's edge and asked, 'You're not seeing Rosie today, then?'

'Alternate Sundays.' Matt sighed. Suddenly shy, he added, 'Actually, I wondered if you'd like to come with me when I take Rosie out next week?'

'Me? Do you think she'd like that?'

'Why wouldn't she?'

'Well, if you don't see that much of each other, shouldn't it be a special time for the two of you? I wouldn't want to be in the way,' she added apologetically.

'Don't you want to come?' Matt sounded hurt and Natty felt a stab of guilt.

She was ashamed to find she wasn't sure if she did want to go. It wasn't that she didn't want to see Rosie; she was an adorable child. But what ought to be a simple afternoon out felt like a big commitment. Was Matt auditioning her for the role of stepmother? Natty wondered. And did she really want the job?

'Oh, I just don't know if I'm any good with kids,' Natty admitted, weakly.

Matt gave her an odd look, as if she'd said she didn't like kids. Natty felt awful. She hadn't meant that at all.

'Well, you don't have to come,' Matt said dejectedly.

In a second it felt as if there was an ocean of distance between them and Natty found it unbearable.

'Of course I want to come!' Natty blurted. 'I guess it's just one of those scary 'first time' things!' Natty made the quotation marks with her fingers, and trilled, 'Just like it was standing on stage . . . I expect I'll feel loads better as soon as I've done it!'

Matt's mood lightened. 'You certainly stood on stage with flying colours.'

'I did, didn't I?' Inwardly, she wondered if she'd handle a day as stepmum with such aplomb.

They'd reached a less crowded

stretch of beach.

'Shall we sit down for a while?' asked Matt.

'It's why I brought my beach towel!' Natty shrugged her bag from her shoulder, shook out her towel and laid it on the sand.

Matt pulled his T-shirt over his head and Natty tried not to gawp at the rippling muscles of his perfectly sculpted torso.

'I should have brought my shorts,' Matt said.

'At least one of us came prepared,' replied Natty.

'You have?' Matt's eyes ran expect-antly up and down her hour-glass figure.

Natty gripped his belt on either side of his hips and turned him away from her.

'No peeking!' While Matt's back was turned, Natty swiftly popped out the dice-shaped buttons of her silk blouse and slipped it off her shoulders. She pushed her striped satin trousers down over her hips and stepped out of them.

Underneath, she was wearing a 1950s-style bikini in sunny yellow with a brightly printed pattern of cocktails, deckchairs, beach umbrellas, orange slices and cherries. There was plenty of room for so many pictures because the bottoms were the size of shorts, with a waistband that came up over her belly button. The top employed just as much fabric, not least in a pair of fully enclosed cups the shape of torpedoes.

'You can look now!' Natty trilled.

Matt turned around and his mouth dropped open.

'Wow! That is what I call a swimsuit!'

From her bag, Natty took a bottle of sun lotion and began spreading it over her arms. 'I don't want to burn!'

'Like me to do your back?' Matt offered, hopefully.

'Yes please!' Lying on her belly, Natty propped herself on one forearm and lifted her red curls from the back of her neck. Matt knelt beside her and tipped a pool of lotion into his palm. The contact of the cool, creamy lotion and the touch of his warm hand between her shoulder blades made her gasp.

'Mmmmmm . . . ' Natty purred like a lioness, as Matt's palm smoothed the lotion up her back and around the curves of her slim shoulders.

She sighed contentedly, wriggling against the towel as his hand slid over the glistening contours of her middle back.

'I see it's not only your feet that are sensitive to touch,' Matt grinned, as he stroked the hollow of her lower back.

'Only the right touch!' Natty warbled. Matt's fingers sent electric currents through her nerves in a way she would never have believed possible. She wished the contact would never have to end. Fortunately, Matt wasn't merely diligent in his slow and thorough application, he took a downright pride in the task. As he massaged deeply into her skin and kneaded the muscles beneath, Natty had never known a pleasure like it!

'Right, this side's done,' said Matt, as

he finished off around her ankles.

Giddy with sensual overload, Natty rolled onto her back, put her hands behind her head and said, decadently, 'You'd better start working your way back up the front, then!'

'I hope I'm going to get the same treatment!' he added, as he smoothed lotion along the fine bone of her shin.

'We'll have to wait and see!' In truth, she was so overwhelmed with pleasure that the thought of rubbing lotion into Matt's rippling muscles was too much for her to even contemplate at the moment!

As Matt's fingers spread lotion into the soft hollow beneath her ribs, Natty felt as if he were stroking her soul.

'I could get used to this pampering!' Natty assured him.

'I'd like to pamper you a lot more,' said Matt. 'Starting with that dinner we haven't had yet. How about this evening?'

Natty sucked her teeth. 'Sorry, I'm rehearsing again tonight.'

'Tomorrow?'

'And tomorrow,' she apologised. 'Then it's the photo shoot. Then it's the recording session . . . '

Matt groaned. 'You know how to keep a guy on tenterhooks, Natty. Do you think there'll ever be a free slot in your diary?'

'Oh, you'll have to ask my agent,' Natty teased. 'If you put a request in writing to Cameron, I'm sure he'll try to fit you in somewhere!'

'I dread to think what it will be like when you're famous,' Matt lamented.

'I'll send you a signed photograph!' Natty assured him.

She wriggled her shoulders into the towel, creating a depression in the sand beneath. With the sun as warm as an oven on her skin, she'd never felt so comfortable.

'At least we're together now,' Natty smiled, suggestively.

'I'd better enjoy the moment, then!' Matt grinned.

A shadow fell across Natty's face as

he leaned over her. Lifting her neck and chin, she formed her lips into a kiss and pushed them eagerly upwards to meet his. Her body already tingling from the sun lotion massage, her heart began drumming in expectation.

The contact when it came was so exquisitely soft, caressing her trembling lips as lightly as a summer breeze, that it took her breath away. Tantalisingly, his lips hovered, barely brushing hers. She stretched her lips upwards, using them to embrace and explore the curve and silky-smooth texture of first his top lip and then the lower.

His lips began probing hers in turn, gently nibbling first her upper lip and then the lower. The moist tip of his tongue joined the gentle exploration, licking her upper lip with a little flick that sent a shiver through her. Stroking his muscular shoulders with her fingertips, she extended her tongue to meet his.

Her breathing quickening, Natty arched her spine away from the towel, twisting and pressing her body against his bare chest. His hand slipped around her flank and into the depression in the small of her back, pulling her to him.

Her eyes closed, lost in the heat of the sun and the heat of their bodies, Natty felt herself growing light-headed, as if she were slipping out of herself and into the most beautiful dream ever. In an illusion as vivid as her everyday life, she was suddenly floating high above the beach.

Far below, on a vast expanse of golden sand empty of everything but them, she saw herself and Matt, his muscular body wrapped around hers, their mouths fused together. They looked like Burt Lancaster and Deborah Kerr in *From Here To Eternity*. She could hear the movie music swelling through the crashing waves and crying seagulls.

At the same time as she was watching from high above, Natty was also hotly present in Matt's arms, every nerve in her body blazing like a forest fire. She'd never believed a kiss could ignite her senses so utterly and so completely blow her mind.

Wow, she thought as she momentarily came back to reality, *if this is living in the moment, who needs a future with all its worries and doubts?*

Never wanting the kiss to end, Natty stroked and squeezed the back of his neck, holding his lips to hers. She thrilled to the touch of his fingertips running up and down the silky groove of her back. As his digits ran over the joints in her spine it was as if he were playing a xylophone, striking beautiful musical notes that chimed right through her.

Natty's only wish was that her skin wasn't sensitive enough to register not just the touch of Matt's hand but the metallic kiss of his wedding ring. She tried to forget Jude's words, but they kept coming back. *It's not the first time they've broken up and you're not the first girlfriend he's had in the meantime. They've always got back together again.*

10

The photographer's studio was in the high street, just a few doors down from Matt's ice-cream parlour on the opposite side of the road. It was a beautiful evening and they decided to go on foot. Natty and Margie walked arm-in-arm in matching white heels and sunglasses, like two Hollywood stars. Margie wore a skirt suit with Dynasty-style shoulder pads. Natty wore a white Fifties dress with a below-the-knee pleated skirt like the one Marilyn Monroe wore in *The Seven Year Itch*. Around her shoulders she wore a powder-blue cashmere shawl fastened with a silver alligator-shaped brooch. In her hair she sported a white carnation. Both women wore white gloves.

Matt brought up the rear, his muscular arms making light work of carrying Natty's guitar case and her hired fur coat in its big zipped bag.

'You've brought him up very well!' Natty quipped.

'Thank you, my dear.' Margie waved her cigarette with aplomb. 'I've always believed a man should be helpful, housetrained and, oh, what's another word beginning with H?'

'Hen-pecked?' Matt grinned.

'That's the one!' Margie squeezed Natty's arm and said, 'Oh, and well dressed . . . like this gentleman up ahead!'

'Yes, look at him!' Natty agreed. 'Take note, Matt, you could learn a thing from Cameron Swoon!'

Cameron was waiting outside the photographers in a sharply tailored black drape suit with a silver Paisley pattern waistcoat. He rang the doorbell and nodded his shiny black quiff at a small window full of framed photos of blushing brides, morning-suited grooms and horse-drawn carriages.

'He mainly does weddings,' Cameron explained, 'but I'm told he does all the local bands, too.'

Natty gazed longingly at the wedding dresses. She felt a stab of pain, too, as she'd almost got as far as booking the photographer for her marriage to David.

Margie said, archly, 'Maybe you'll be booking this chap again, before too long, Natty.'

Natty gave her landlady a conspiratorial wink and said, 'If I do, I hope you'll be there!'

'Close your ears, Matt,' said Margie. 'This is girls' talk!'

Matt looked at the window display less enthusiastically. 'This is the guy who did my wedding pictures. No happy ever after there, unfortunately.'

'I hope it hasn't given you an aversion to confetti!' Natty trilled, nervously.

'Oh no.' Matt grinned. 'Just an aversion to Jen!'

The door was opened by a tall, skeletal young man with short black hair and the pallor of a man who spent a lot of his time in a darkened studio. He glanced at Cameron's suit and the white outfits of Natty and Margie and quipped, 'Bit late in the day for a wedding, isn't it? Just joking! I'm Andy. Come in!'

They followed Andy down a narrow corridor into a square room with black walls and ceiling. Cameron said, 'It's good of you to fit us in out of hours.'

'I had to swap a few things around,' said Andy, 'but when you mentioned Gary Morris . . . '

'As I said on the phone, I cannae promise anything,' said Cameron. 'But I know Gary was unhappy with the guy who shot the 3-Dom cover. Great talent, terrible attitude. He charged like a rhino, too.'

Andy ran an appreciative eye over Natty's outfit. 'You said post-war glamour, so I thought we could take a couple in front of this backdrop of New York skyscrapers, then maybe a few in front of a chintzy red curtain — a cabaret kind of look?'

Andy opened a door. 'If you need to change, Natty, you can use the office, through there.'

While Andy set up his camera and tripod, Margie remarked, 'This takes me back to my Coconut Crunch days!'

Cameron gazed at her with a raised eyebrow. 'That was you? I've been thinking all this time that you looked somehow familiar.'

★ ★ ★

Natty had never been the star of a photo shoot before but she was in her element. With no sensation of time passing in the windowless room, she struck pose after pose — in her snowball fur coat, in her Fifties dress, standing, sitting daintily on a bistro chair, reclining on a chaise lounge.

Andy stoked her vanity, dancing around her with light meters and lenses, adjusting lights and reflectors.

'Beautiful, beautiful!' Andy encouraged as he crouched over his camera. 'The camera loves you!'

Natty loved the buzzing and whirring camera just as much. The cascading lightning strikes of the flash guns were like sunshine on a butterfly's wings; they gave her energy and made her feel alive in a way she'd never felt before.

Andy rubbed his chin thoughtfully. 'Do you know what that dress needs, Natty?'

He plugged in a desk fan and positioned it on the floor a little in front of her. 'Have you ever seen *The Seven Year Itch?*'

'I know what to do!'

As a warm wind whooshed up her legs, Natty pressed the front of her skirt to her knees with one hand while the hem billowed up like a parachute around her pink suspenders and the tops of her light tan stockings.

'Do I look like Marilyn?' Natty giggled, as she eyed Matt.

Matt was too entranced to answer.

When the shoot was finally over, Andy looked at his watch and laughed. 'Have you seen the time, guys? It's midnight. I thought we'd only be here an hour!'

'Time flies when you're having fun!' Natty giggled.

'It does when you're looking through a lens at a model as beautiful as you,' Andy said with a note of awe. Turning to Cameron, he said, 'When do you need these?'

'First thing Friday morning,' Cameron said briskly. 'The best six mounted, ten by twelve, the rest on a contact sheet. Oh, and Natty, I have a wee bit of good news I almost forgot to tell you. I was going to post the pictures and demo to Gary, but I must have given him such a hard sell he wants to meet you in person. Are you free to come with me to his house on Saturday?'

★   ★   ★

'I'm starting to feel like a star!' exclaimed Natty, as Matt drove her to the recording session in his pink and cream Chevy the following evening.

'You certainly look like one!' Matt grinned. 'I bet those pictures will look fantastic.'

'And you're going to see Gary Morris

on Saturday!' Margie enthused from the back seat. 'I bet he gives you a record deal on the spot!'

'That's if the demo is any good,' Natty replied. 'I feel almost too nervous to sing!'

'We're all here to cheer you on,' said Jase, who was sitting with Margie in the back.

'Only cheer if it's good!' Natty said anxiously. 'That's why I want you with me, to let me know if it sounds as good as something you'd play as a DJ.'

'It sounded good at the rehearsals,' Jase assured her. 'It's got that Fifties retro twist but it's bang up to the minute pop at the same time. I think there's something magical about that *Second Chance* song.'

'It's the lyric,' Margie said, emphatically. 'Who wouldn't want a second chance, eh, Matt?'

Suddenly shy, Natty stole a tiny sideways glance at Matt to check his reaction. Her heart leapt when his chiselled cheek coloured and he gave her the smallest and shyest of smiles.

Turning to her side window, Natty began singing the chorus of her song, as if she were having a last minute rehearsal, but hoping Matt would get the message: *'Everybody deserves a second chance . . . yeah, yeah, yeah.'*

The studio was in a converted brick barn on the rural outskirts of the town. Matt swung the big Chevy onto the crunchy gravel of an enclosed court-yard. Through a tall glass wall where the barn door would once have been, Natty saw the Bop Tones setting up their equipment under the impassive eye of the drape-suited Cameron.

The studio had a bright, clean, modern look. Compared to the infor-mal rehearsals in Margie's living room, the evening's mission suddenly had a very serious and professional feel. Natty wasn't intimidated, though. Despite an exciting tingling in her nerves, she felt confident about *Second Chance* and another two songs of hers that she'd rehearsed.

Duke and the Bop Tones spent their days playing on records by big-name singers who graced the charts. As Jase had said, they'd brought a modern sensibility to Natty's music while preserving its vintage charm.

More than that, Natty was enjoying every moment of her preparation for fame. As she strolled regally into the studio, one arm linked through Margie's and the other linked through Matt's, while Jase carried her guitar case, she felt like a star arriving with her entourage!

Duke leaned into the microphone in the centre of the studio and said in his echoing Elvis voice, 'And here comes the lady of the moment, the uh-huh girl with the golden voice, the swinging, singing sensation, the uh, wonderful Miss Natty Smalls!'

They recorded 'live' with the band playing while Natty sang because, as Duke said, 'That's the way Elvis did it. And if it's good enough for the King it's, uh, good enough for us!'

With the drums thundering away

behind her and Duke's electric guitar adding a grungy depth to her own, Natty felt as if she were surfing a tidal wave of sound. It was an exhilarating, transporting experience. So well rehearsed she didn't have to think about her playing or singing, Natty was barely aware of doing either of those things. She just locked eyes with Matt, where he was watching, transfixed through the glass window of the control room, opened her soul and let the song's message pour out of her heart and into his.

Natty struck a final reverberating chord and as the ringing sound decayed slowly into the ether, she felt as though she were gently parachuting back to earth. Because for the previous three minutes she'd felt as if she were flying.

Back on the solid ground of reality, Natty lifted her guitar in the air and screamed with delight. In the control room, Matt, Margie and Jase clapped and cheered. Duke leaned into his microphone and said in his Elvis voice, 'If that don't turn Gary Morris on then he, uh, ain't got no switches!'

Before they left the studio, Natty asked Duke to burn the song onto a CD for her. With a CD marker she inscribed it:

To Matt,
Everybody deserves a second chance.
Natty

She drew the 'y' at the end of her name as a heart with a tail that looped under the rest of the word, slipped the disc into a sachet and pressed it into Matt's hands.

'When it's sold a million you'll have the very first copy!' Natty whispered so only he could hear.

'I'll treasure it forever!' promised Matt, holding the CD to his heart. 'And now it's recorded, hopefully you'll finally have an evening free so we can have that dinner I've been waiting for.'

11

For their date at The Aquarium, Matt wore a 1950s American-made suit in brown wool with a white fleck. His white shirt had two buttons undone at his throat and the wide pointed collar sat outside the equally wide lapels of his jacket. His shoes had thick black crepe soles and dazzling white leather uppers defined with sharp black piping.

'Nice suit!' said Natty, as she skipped down the stairs and found him waiting by the front door.

'Well, with Cameron always looking so smart, I thought I'd better up my game!'

Natty slipped her arms inside his open jacket and wrapped them around his muscular torso. She propped her chin on his bulging chest. 'Don't worry, Matt, you've got something special that Cameron will never have.'

'And that is . . . ?' Matt inquired with a smile.

'Me!' Natty trilled, playfully.

'That's good enough for me! And you look amazing, Natty, as always,' he said appreciatively.

'What, this old thing?' With her hair pinned up like Brigitte Bardot in a tower of swirls atop her crown, Natty was wearing a burnt orange mini-dress first sold at Mary Quant's boutique Bazaar in the early Sixties. Cut squarely across her throat and four inches above her knee, she'd teamed it with opaque white tights and white heels with a winkle-picker toe for the monochrome look of the Mod era.

'I haven't even looked at your clothes yet,' Matt grinned. 'I was talking about your face!'

'So what about the clothes?' Natty did a twirl.

'Mmmm.' Matt nodded his approval. 'You should wear short skirts more often . . . maybe even shorter!'

'How about this short?' Natty playfully

hiked her hem up another two inches.

'Bit shorter!' Matt encouraged.

'This short?' She hiked it another inch.

'Getting there . . . ' He was starting to breathe heavily.

Natty laughed and lowered her hem to its rightful place. 'Any shorter and I don't think I'd be getting out the door!'

'You're probably right!' Matt grinned.

★ ★ ★

The Aquarium was undoubtedly the most stunning place Natty had ever eaten in. From a bar and reception lounge in a grand Victorian pavilion, a curved staircase descended into a shadowy dining room. The blue and green-tinted light constantly shifted and swirled because it was coming from irregularly shaped glass panels in walls faced with rough stone. In the blue water behind the glass swam shimmering shoals of rainbow-coloured tropical fish, seahorses, spiky-faced catfish and even small sharks.

'Wow!' said Natty, as they followed a waiter down the red-carpeted staircase. 'It's like going under the sea!'

'I bet you've been to a few fancy restaurants, going out with David,' Matt said, as he held her hand.

'One or two, but I've never been to one like this!'

She'd never been to one with a man who made her heart race like Matt did, either.

Looking back, Natty realised David had lavished everything on her except his full attention. His phone was never out of his hand as he kept round-the-clock tabs on his many businesses. When they were out together, half his time was spent greeting the celebrities or business people he knew. Towards the end of their time together, Natty had started to feel like little more than another of the expensive accessories he'd picked up to enhance his image but which he actually cared very little for.

Matt, by contrast, always looked at

her as if she were the most wonderful thing he'd ever seen.

She felt the same way about Matt. She wished she could tell him how she felt. Still not quite having the nerve, she contented herself with giving his hand an extra special squeeze.

While they waited for their food, and a shoal of iridescent fish swam past their table, Matt asked, 'Are you nervous about meeting Gary Morris tomorrow?'

'Yes . . . and no.' Natty smiled blithely, a mix of emotion crossing her face.

Matt gazed at her in disbelief. 'I'd be terrified if it were me!'

'I'm excited,' Natty admitted. 'And I know I should be feeling nervous. But, for some reason, I just feel incredibly calm about the whole thing. It sounds big-headed, and I don't mean it to sound like that, but for the first time in my life it feels as if everything is going to fall into place.'

'You've got a fantastic demo,' Matt agreed.

'It's not just that,' Natty said, thoughtfully. She gazed earnestly into his eyes. 'Have you ever had a moment when a little voice inside your head says, 'Yes, this is meant to be'?'

Matt gazed back at her, his eyes shimmering pools of blue.

'Oh yes, I've heard that voice,' he answered dreamily. 'I hear it every time I look at you.'

Natty glanced away, for a moment not daring to meet his eyes. Then, with her heart beginning to drum in her ears, she did meet his gaze. 'It's funny you should say that . . . ' she said.

Matt slid his hand across the tablecloth and put it over hers. His touch sent a tingle through her.

'Maybe we should act on it,' Matt whispered.

Almost as if the words were coming from somebody else, Natty heard herself murmur, 'Maybe we should.'

★　★　★

Matt parked in the little yard at the back of the house. Holding hands, they ran through the back door into the kitchen. The light was off and neither reached for the switch. Moonlight flowed through the window and lay like pools of spilt milk on the worktops. That was all the light they needed.

As Matt clicked the door shut behind them, Natty turned towards him. Matt stepped into her arms. He clutched her waist to his, lifting her onto her toes. Her body melted into an arch against him. Her head fell back. Her mouth fell open. His lips closed over hers.

Like dancers waltzing without music, they crossed the kitchen in circles — lips together, then apart, then together again.

Her back found the edge of the breakfast bar. His stomach, hard and rippling with muscle, pressed against hers, pinning her in place. His kissing became urgent, hungry, ravenous. She pressed her mouth upwards into his. Closing her eyes, she sank into a world of touch and taste. His lips, moist and burning. His palms and fingers pressing through her dress as they ran slowly and smoothly up and down her back.

Her eager fingers explored the spiky, close-cropped hair on the back of his head. She examined the contours of his skull, then the smoothness of his neck. Her hands moved lower. Through the wool of his jacket she felt the thick cords of muscle in his back.

His arms enfolded her. His biceps were as thick as the bodies of giant snakes. Yet his touch was so gentle. His caress made her feel as precious as vintage china.

Eventually, Matt eased his lips from hers.

Natty was breathing hard, as if she'd been running. Having forgotten where she was, she looked up, startled, into his smiling eyes. His face was close, poised to kiss her again. But his eyes were glowing with a new idea.

In a hopeful whisper, Matt said, 'Shall we go somewhere more comfortable?'

Fevered images swirled in Natty's mind — a tangle of clothes, sheets, arms, legs. She felt like a fire that could never be put out. The moment felt like a runaway train that could never be stopped. But . . .

Trembling all over, Natty put two fingers on his lips. She eased his face back from hers to give herself some breathing space. He relaxed his hold on her and looked at her, quizzically.

'Oh, Matt,' Natty said quietly. 'There's something I need to tell you.'

'You used to be a man?' Matt blurted.

'What?' Natty demanded in horror.

'Just a joke!' Matt grinned.

'Bad joke!' Natty reprimanded him with distaste.

'Sorry!' Matt chuckled nervously. 'What, then?'

Suddenly shy, Natty finally confessed. 'I, um, believe in waiting until marriage.'

Hoping he wouldn't be able to see her reddening cheeks in the moonlight and shadows, Natty watched his face closely while he worked out what she meant.

'You mean you're . . . '

'Completely innocent and untouched!'

Matt grinned giddily. 'Well, we'd better get married, then!'

Natty laughed. She knew he was joking, after all, they'd only just met. The word 'married' still gave her a jolt, though, and a stab of pain. She hadn't realised until now how scarred David Royale's lies had left her. That wasn't Matt's fault, though, and she hoped he didn't see the flinch behind her laughter.

'I mean it!' Matt grinned.

'I know you do,' Natty smiled knowingly, ' . . . at the moment! But will you still want to marry me tomorrow? Or next week? Or in . . . oh, I don't know . . . a month's time?'

'Of course I will. I'll prove it, too.'

'How?'

'By asking you tomorrow . . . and in a month's time, and in six months, or however long I have to wait until you say yes.'

'We'll wait and see then!' Natty giggled.

'Do we have to wait for this, too?' Matt leaned forward and kissed her lips so softly her heart almost stopped.

'No, we don't have to wait for that.' Natty pulled him towards her and kissed him back.

'Thank goodness for that!' He kissed her again. Their lips lingered, but more lightly and gently than before. They held and caressed each other, tenderly and less urgently. Their breathing quickened, but not too much. Her body simmered, but within the controllable range.

And, somehow, without the frenzy and without the nagging fear in the back of her head that she might do something she would regret in the morning, their slow sensual enjoyment of each other was all the more exquisite.

At length, they both came up for air once more. Natty felt as warm and gooey as melted caramel in his arms. She felt safe and profoundly relaxed, too, in a way she'd never felt with David or any other boyfriend. Normally in a clinch Natty was on perpetual Wandering Hands Alert. It was exciting, but constantly defending her boundaries against persistent incursions was far from relaxing — it was exhausting.

With Matt, for the first time in her life, it didn't feel like that. His hands weren't boisterous intruders to be watched, they were guests who knew how to behave themselves, guests of the sort she hoped would never go home, because she knew she'd miss them unbearably.

For a long time, they gazed unselfconsciously into each other's eyes and what she saw mirrored the contentment she felt inside.

Softy, Matt whispered, 'You do know I love you, Natty?'

The word jolted her, the way 'married' had earlier. It was strange, Natty reflected, how the language of touch could be so relaxing and the language of words so unsettling. She guessed it was because the former spoke to her heart and soul, which were always so trusting, while the latter spoke to her mind — and her mind was always so full of doubts and fears.

Sometimes Natty wished she didn't have a mind; like a nagging parent, it always seemed to be stopping her body having fun. But, grudgingly, she had to admit the old killjoy kept her out of trouble. She tried to ignore the little warning bell disturbing her physical state of bliss. But it wouldn't go away.

Gathering her courage, Natty took a deep breath and said softly, 'There's one thing that's bothering me.'

Matt's face creased into a question mark. Natty peeled his left hand off her hip. She took his third finger between her finger and thumb and lifted the hand up between their faces where they could both see it.

Matt looked at the hand, confused.

'If it's really all over between you and Jen,' Natty said quietly, 'why do you still wear your ring?'

For a moment, Matt looked at her

blankly. Then he smiled. He waggled his ring finger.

'Take it off,' he said, simply.

It was Natty's turn to look confused. 'What?'

'Take the ring off for me.'

Natty gave him a sideways look, wondering if he was serious. Then she laughed and took hold of the gold wedding band. She gave it a tug. It moved, but only with the play in the flesh of his finger as his skin furrowed up around the joint. Giggling, she adjusted her grip and tried again.

'Tight, isn't it!' Natty giggled. Using both hands, one holding his hand and the other making a fist around his ring finger, she twisted and turned the ring, trying to loosen it. Only the flesh on his finger moved.

To Natty, the ring suddenly represented Jen, obstinately refusing to be prised from Matt's life. *Well, if you want a fight* . . . Natty mentally rolled up her sleeves for a showdown.

Determined to free Matt from his

marital chain, she turned her back on him and clamped his arm under her armpit to give her some leverage. Baring her teeth, she braced her elbow against his stomach. She tugged his wrist in one direction and his finger in the other.

'Aaaagh!' Matt yelled.

'Shhhh!' Natty giggled. She clamped her hand over his mouth. 'Your mum'll wonder what we're doing!'

Matt rubbed his finger. The skin had turned white in places and red in others, but the gold ring remained stubbornly in place.

'Does that answer your question?' he asked with a pained grin on his face.

'Have you tried butter?' Natty asked.

'Yep.'

'Oil?'

'Yep.'

'Hmmmm.' Natty rubbed her chin. 'And that's really the only reason you're still wearing it? Because you can't get it off?'

'Can you think of a better reason?'

Matt spluttered. 'I've been trying to get it off for years, but it just gets tighter.'

'Well,' said Natty, 'if you really want to prove you love me, there's only one thing for it — you'll have to go to the fire station and have it cut off.'

'My finger?' Matt yelped. He clutched his digit protectively.

'No, you big goof, the ring!'

12

'He's here!' hollered Margie. In a white tailored suit and matching hat with an enormous brim, Margie looked like a mother of the bride — and was just as nervous. She took a final deep drag on her cigarette and stubbed it out in an ashtray shaped like Elvis's profile.

Natty ran to the living room window in time to see Cameron stepping out of a sleek black Jaguar. The Teddy Boy was as immaculately dressed as ever in a pale yellow waistcoat over an ivory silk shirt and maroon ribbon tie. Around his biceps he wore expanding silver rings to keep his cuffs at the right length. The car looked brand new. Natty hoped it was an omen of affluence to come.

'You don't mind me coming, do you?' Margie fretted.

'Of course not!' Natty gave her landlady a hug. She was enjoying being part of a big extended family. She hoped Margie would always be in her life.

'Or me?' Jase asked nervously. As an aspiring DJ, meeting a big time producer like Gary Morris was the thrill of a lifetime.

'The more the merrier!' Natty trilled.

Cameron rang the doorbell.

'I'll get it!' called Matt, as he came clattering down the stairs at speed.

★ ★ ★

The cream leather seats of the Jag were the height of luxury and the big car ate up the motorway with barely a purr from its powerful engine.

'I could get used to travelling in style!' Natty preened, in the passenger seat.

'You'd better get used to it,' said Cameron, from behind the steering wheel. 'If Gary likes your demo it will be chauffeured limos and private jets all the way.'

The journey flew by and it seemed like no time before they were cruising along a leafy avenue so exclusive that the houses couldn't even be seen behind tall brick walls and screens of mature trees. Cameron swung the Jag off the road and crunched to a halt on a patch of gravel outside a set of tall iron gates. The Scot turned in his seat to look at Natty, and Matt, Margie and Jase in the backseat. He looked serious and uncharacteristically ill at ease.

'Before we go in,' Cameron said quietly, 'there's something you should know about Gary. The laddie's a genius and he's had a lot of success in a short time. The combination of those things can make a person seem . . . well, a wee bit strange. Sometimes he can seem very intense. At other times he might seem distracted, as if he's not listening to you. Some people find it disconcerting, but it's just because he moves on very quickly in his own head. The best thing to do is act normally. If you've got what he wants, which I believe you have, Natty, he'll be interested, believe me.'

The pep talk over, Cameron lowered his window and spoke into an intercom. The gates swung open and they drove up a long, winding drive, through immaculately manicured gardens to the biggest private residence Natty had ever seen.

'Wow,' breathed Matt.

'You see where a couple of hit records can get you?' Cameron said with a raised eyebrow.

He parked beside a scarlet Ferrari outside a covered porch supported by columns on a scale normally only found in Roman architecture. Matt took Natty's guitar case from the boot along with the sketch pad in which he'd drawn some ideas for album covers. Jase collected the photographs in their folded mounts. Natty slipped her hand into Margie's for moral support. Despite what she'd told Matt about feeling calm about the meeting, the size of Gary Morris's house and gardens was suddenly making her very nervous indeed!

Cameron rang the doorbell and Natty listened to the thumping of her heart.

The door finally opened and a young man built like a bear was hugging Cameron like a long lost brother. 'Cameron! So good to see you again!'

'You, too, Gary.' The always self-contained Teddy Boy looked stiff and uncomfortable within the embrace. As Gary's arms relaxed their grip, Cameron said, in a tone of relief, 'Allow me to introduce Miss Natty Smalls.'

Cameron had told Natty to dress like a star, adding, 'Not that I need to tell you that, lassie — you always look like a star.'

Natty had taken him at his word. She was wearing a waspwaist, swirl-skirted replica 1950s rock'n'roll dress in fuchsia pink with a pattern of white hearts. The dress was sleeveless so she'd teamed it with a tiny pale pink cardigan. The cardigan was matched by a diaphanous pink headscarf, knotted under her chin, with her red hair rolled up over the front into a towering pompadour and cascading out of the back in rows of carefully rolled curls. Her shiny stilettos matched the pink in her dress and her sunglasses were in the shape of two hearts the colour of her hair.

Gary Morris, by contrast, looked like a beach bum. His mousy hair was dishevelled. His T-shirt and baggy, knee-length shorts were so faded it was hard to guess what colour they had been originally. On a pair of enormous bare feet he wore leather sandals that appeared on the verge of falling apart. Only a big pair of glasses with thick black rims gave the producer a studious look and an air of deep intelligence.

He held out his hand. Natty took it apprehensively, and he stared into her sunglasses with such intensity that she felt he was staring into her soul.

With a formality at odds with his scruffy appearance, Gary said, 'I'm very pleased to meet you Miss Smalls.'

'Likewise,' Natty breathed.

'In you come, then!' Without glancing at the others, Gary turned abruptly and stomped into the house.

Cameron motioned them to follow and led the nervous party into a study three times the size of Margie's living room.

Four large leather sofas were grouped casually around a circular glass coffee table. French doors opened onto a palatial paved terrace and, beyond that, a sparkling blue swimming pool could just be seen.

Gary hurled his bulk onto a sofa beneath a vastly blown-up photograph of himself posing with the three girls from 3-Dom on what appeared to be a tropical beach.

'What have we got, then?' Gary asked Cameron, with sudden casualness.

'First,' said Cameron, 'let me show you some photographs.'

Gary swung his feet off the sofa and was immediately completely focused on the glossy prints that Cameron laid one by one on the coffee table.

'Oh, these are good,' Gary murmured. 'Why didn't we get this guy to shoot the 3-Dom cover? This one in particular: now that's a CD cover.'

'Gorgeous, isn't she?' Cameron said smoothly. 'Now, Matthew here has come up with some album cover concepts that I think really accentuate Natty's retro style.'

Cameron showed Gary Matt's designs.

'That's exactly what I would do.' The producer nodded. He shot Matt an intense stare. 'Where did you train?'

Matt's chiselled cheeks reddened. 'Oh, um, er . . . '

Natty put her arm around Matt's muscular shoulders and stated proudly, 'Matt's a self-taught genius!'

'Good enough for me!' Gary grinned with approval. 'Let's hear some music!'

Natty's stomach tightened nervously as Cameron opened what appeared to be a highly polished antique cabinet to reveal a state of the art sound system. He slipped her CD in the tray and the intro to *Second Chance* filled the room. Natty could barely believe how professional it sounded, thanks to the Bop Tones' expert backing. What it sounded like to Gary, though, she barely dared to imagine, and the producer offered no clue.

Throwing himself back on the sofa with his chin pointing at the ceiling, Gary screwed his eyes tightly shut while he listened. His body was as immobile as a statue. Barely daring to move, Natty gripped Matt's hand with her left hand and Margie's hand with her right.

As the final note faded, Gary pulled a zapper from between the cushions of his sofa and stopped the CD. He leaned forward and stared intensely at Natty for what felt like an eternity, before pronouncing solemnly, 'That is exactly what I'm looking for.'

'Oh, Natty! I knew it!' Margie squealed in utter delight.

Natty turned to her right and Margie hugged her. She turned to her left and Matt hugged her.

Gary grinned gleefully. 'That sounds like a single, wouldn't you say, Cameron?'

The corner of Cameron's lips flickered into a smile as he said, 'That's what I've been trying to tell you . . . '

'This calls for some tea!' Gary declared. 'Pop in the kitchen, Cameron, and stick the kettle on.'

Natty was taken aback by the casual rudeness of the order but Cameron left the room with no sign of unease. Natty guessed Gary's abrupt manner was just part of the odd behaviour Cameron had warned them about.

'Let's listen to it again, and the rest of the tracks,' said Gary. He pointed the zapper and as the sound of Natty's guitar filled the room once more, lapsed back into an apparent trance.

By the time the demo was finished, Cameron was back with a tray of teacups.

Gary stared at Natty. 'Cameron tells me you're working for a newspaper. How do you feel about giving that up for a life of international celebrity?'

Natty gave the producer a sideways look. She could only imagine he was joking, although his completely straight face suggested otherwise.

'I guess I could manage!' she replied, nervously.

Gary's face didn't flicker. 'I'm serious, Natty. It's not just about writing songs. There will be rehearsals, meetings, videos, promotion.' He jerked a thumb at the photo of himself with 3-Dom. 'The girls haven't had more than three or four weekends off in the past two years. Next year they're doing America, which will be even more full-on, because that's the commitment it takes to make it big in this business.'

'I'm game if you are!' Natty warbled.

'And your boyfriend . . . ?' Gary stared intently at Matt. 'How do you feel about Natty putting in so much work?'

The word 'boyfriend' gave Natty a jolt. Was that what Matt was now? Natty had barely got her head around the idea that they had started going out together. Neither had she considered until that moment that embracing life as a singing sensation was about more than her; it would have implications for her relationship with Matt, too.

Suddenly, Natty couldn't look at him. Would he resent her devoting so much time to her career? Would he be jealous of her success? At a time when things between her and Matt were still so new and fragile, standing on the verge of a recording contract suddenly felt a lot scarier than she'd expected.

To her immense relief, Matt's hand squeezed hers.

'Whatever makes Natty happy is fine by me,' he grinned.

'Oh, Matt!' Overwhelmed with love, Natty threw her arms around Matt and kissed him passionately on the lips.

Gary cleared his throat impatiently. Embarrassed, Natty turned her attention back to the producer.

'I don't know if Cameron has explained the set-up, but before I can offer you a contract I'll have to go to

London and talk money with the record label. Don't worry, it's just a formality. A courtesy, really. Cameron, how soon can you get me a meeting with Alan?'

The corner of Cameron's mouth flickered into a smile. 'If you'll forgive my forwardness, Gary, I've booked the three of us for lunch on Monday.'

Gary looked startled, then pointed at Cameron and said, 'You know me so well!' Abruptly, he leapt to his feet. 'I'm sorry I can't sit and talk, but I have another meeting. Can I leave Cameron to call you with the details on Monday?'

The producer thrust out his hand and said solemnly, 'I'm so looking forward to working with you, Miss Smalls.'

'And me you! Thank you so, so much!'

Impulsively, Natty flung her arms around Gary and planted a pink Cupid's bow lip print on his cheek. Matt and Jase slapped palms in a high five.

'And thank you, Cameron!' Margie flung her arms around the Teddy Boy and planted an appreciative smacker on his startled lips. Cameron's eyebrows shot towards his quiff as if they were on elastic and, for the first time since he'd come into her life, Natty saw a red flush come to his normally pallid cheeks.

13

In the small hours of that night, Natty lay in bed awake and wondered if she'd ever sleep again. The meeting with Gary Morris kept replaying over and over in her mind. He loved her music! She was going to be a star! Or was she? Natty kept reminding herself that it all depended on the meeting in London between Gary, Cameron and the record company. She wouldn't know for certain until Monday evening, which meant she'd be on tenterhooks for two whole days!

What time Natty finally got to sleep she didn't know. But when she woke on Sunday morning, the same things were still chasing each other around her head. Two whole days until she'd know if Gary had the go-ahead to record her! Natty didn't know how she'd get through until then.

Fortunately, she had another appointment to occupy her mind. As she went through her morning routine, as jittery as a bride before a wedding, Natty wondered what she should wear for her first day out with Matt's daughter.

Deeming something practical was in order, she chose a pair of calf-length pink pedal pushers, to go with her pink and black sneakers. She teamed the trousers with a vintage white cotton blouse delicately embroidered with a pattern of blue cornflowers on the front. Feeling like Doris Day, she pinned a large and fragrant white lily in her hair.

Singing *Once I Had A Secret Love*, Natty skipped down the stairs to find Matt waiting for her in the hall.

'Wow, you look fantastic!'

'So do you,' Natty said truthfully.

Matt looked down at his clothes, puzzled. 'I always wear jeans and a T-shirt.'

Natty wrapped her arms around him and propped her chin on his muscular chest. 'It's not your clothes that look fantastic,' she assured him.

'I've boiled your egg,' said Matt. 'Sorry to rush you, but I don't want to be late picking up Rosie.'

'Of course not!' Natty hurried through to the kitchen. 'I'm glad you invited me. I'm really looking forward to it.'

She was, too, although secretly Natty was even more nervous about spending the day with Matt and Rosie than she had been about meeting Gary Morris. It felt like another audition, only this one had even more depending on it and she was by no means as confident about the outcome. Her experience of parent-ing was zero. What if Matt decided she'd be a lousy stepmother? What if Rosie didn't like her?

But most worrying of all — and Natty was almost too ashamed to admit the doubt even to herself — what if she didn't enjoy playing stepmum?

As an only child, Natty never had any little sisters to look after. She had no big sisters with babies of their own.

She'd never gone as gooey over other people's children as some of her friends did. In fact, Natty was usually too scared to pick up another woman's baby in case it spilled something gooey over her! In Natty's book, vintage clothes and sticky kids simply did not equal a relaxing time.

'Ready?' grinned Matt, a large plastic cool-bag in his arms.

'Ready!' Natty dumped her plate and empty eggcup in the sink and chased her big handsome man down the hall to the front door.

On the steps outside the house, Natty stopped dead. At the kerb, where she expected Matt's mighty 57 Chevrolet to be parked was a rickety little Citroen 2CV that, by comparison, looked as if it had been made of folded paper and bicycle wheels. The many oddly shaped panels were painted in contrasting shades of pink and yellow. On the doors, in big frothy lettering, was the legend *Posh Knickers* above an illustration of some black lace confection.

'What is that?' Natty asked, in astonishment.

'Mum's car. We're borrowing it.'

'Where's your car?'

Matt looked sheepish. 'The Chevy's actually the ice-cream parlour's car. Jen owns half of it, and she's using it today to visit her mum and dad.'

Jen, Natty thought bitterly — *will that woman's shadow ever be out of my life? No,* she thought sadly, *it won't, not as long as Jen and Matt share a child. That relationship is for life.*

'Still, we've got the better deal,' Matt enthused. 'I'd rather have Rosie for the day than a car!'

He looked so proud and happy to be seeing his daughter that Natty was ashamed of herself for putting their transport above the real reason for their excursion.

Taking a fresh look at the car, Natty decided the little Citroen actually looked quite fun. While Matt put his cool-bag of sandwiches and ice-cream in the boot, Natty skipped around the vehicle, marvelling at its bulbous headlights, which stood out like frog's eyes, and wheel arches as flared as a clown car's. She reckoned the car must be thirty years old and based on a design little changed since the Sixties. In its way, it was as much of a vintage classic as the Chevy.

'Do we have to wind it up before we get in?' Natty grinned.

'No — just stick your feet through the floor and run!'

The doors slammed like two metal trays banging together and Natty found herself rubbing elbows with Matt in the narrow interior. Even the window didn't wind down like a normal window, Natty discovered — it folded outwards from a hinge at the top.

'I should 'ave worn a beret and striped T-shirt!' Natty said in a French accent.

'Zare are some French knickers in ze boot if Mademoiselle fancies trying zem on later,' replied Matt. In his own accent, he added, 'Really there are

— there's a whole load of Mum's stock!'

'In your dreams, Monsieur!' Natty returned, primly.

With the engine sounding as though it were powered by rubber bands, Matt drove swiftly through the town to a street lined on both sides with small Victorian terraced houses. He parked behind the tail fins of the pink and cream Chevy, and Natty looked up at the house Matt had shared with Jen.

She felt a stab of sadness on his behalf. It was a neat and pretty home, with a bright green front door and window frames — the kind of place where any young couple would be proud to begin their married life.

Natty could well imagine how happy Matt and Jen must have been when they first moved in, never dreaming that, within a few short years, one of them would be living there on their own.

'Do you want to wait here?' Matt asked awkwardly.

Natty wasn't sure whether he wanted her to stay out of the way or whether he wanted her to go with him for support.

'I'd better stay here,' Natty said, nervously. For a moment, Matt's face made her wonder if she'd made the right choice. With a sigh, he climbed out of the car and closed the tinny door.

She watched him walk up the short path, admiring the breadth of his shoulders and the narrowness of his hips. She wondered if he'd use a key to let himself in, and braced herself for the stab of jealousy that would cause. To her relief, he rang the doorbell and waited on the step.

The green door opened and Jen emerged, her raven hair tied back in a sleek ponytail. In one arm she held Rosie, who was wearing a yellow sundress with a red and green pattern of wrapped sweets. In her other hand, Jen held a child's booster seat for the car.

Matt took Rosie in his arms and for a

moment stood talking to Jen, he grinning nervously, she tense and unsmiling. Natty felt queasy, like a voyeur, but couldn't look away. Jealously, she looked for signs of a lingering spark between the two. She found herself studying Jen's tall, slim figure and lustrous black hair, comparing herself to the woman Matt had once loved enough to marry and have a baby with.

Natty wondered how she measured up. Jen was an attractive woman. According to Matt, she was a good jiver, too.

To Natty's horror, Jen cast a sudden narrowed-eye look at the Citroen and its occupant. Matt looked her way, too, and Natty was certain they were talking about her. Under Jen's scrutiny, she filled with guilt.

Poised on the step of the house they'd shared, Matt, Jen and Rosie looked like such a perfect family, they could have been in an advert for mortgages. Natty felt as if she was breaking them up. She knew she was being irrational — Matt had split from Jen before she came along. But she couldn't help wondering if he would be making more of an effort to repair his marriage if she hadn't come along.

Should he be making more effort? Natty asked herself. *Am I encouraging him to ruin Jen's life . . . and little Rosie's?*

Natty felt dwarfed by the questions. Fortunately, she didn't have time to dwell on them.

The front door closed and Matt began walking back to the car with Rosie sitting in the crook of his arm. They were all smiles, the proud dad and the adoring daughter, and the sight of them sent a surge of love through Natty.

An image flashed into her mind of the big grinning man carrying another child on his shoulders and leading a third by the hand — Natty's children.

Would that be so wrong? Natty wondered. It didn't *feel* wrong. But how would she feel in Jen's shoes?

Matt began strapping Rosie into the back seat. Natty twisted around to make a fuss of the child. She was determined to not let Matt or Rosie see a hint of her inner doubts. It was their day and she was determined not to spoil it for them.

Rosie giggled with delight and stretched her hands towards the flower in Natty's hair.

'You want my lily?' Natty asked. She got out and climbed into the back. 'Here, let me pin it in your hair. Shall I ride in the back with you?'

'Yes!' grinned Rosie.

'We'll be like two queens in a carriage!' Natty said in her sing-song voice. She gave Matt an imperious tap on the shoulder and said in her poshest voice, 'Drive on, driver, and don't spare the horses!'

* * *

Matt drove out of town to a quieter stretch of coastline. From a rough gravel car park, a sandy path led between grassy dunes to a wide cove. Surprisingly, only a handful of family groups dotted the sunny beach.

'I used to come here as a kid, with my mum and dad,' Natty recalled as they walked towards a quiet spot.

As they knelt on beach towels and unpacked their picnic, Natty felt as if she'd slipped back in time. Except the perspective had changed. Natty was no longer a giggling four-year-old, dropping crumbs in the sand and looking up at two giant parents. As she gazed at Rosie, gambolling in her sundress, Natty realised that she'd become . . . the parent?

It was a disconcerting feeling, as if she'd woken up in a strange room and couldn't remember how she'd got there. All her life she'd dreamed about romance — tall, handsome men; a big white wedding; a happy-ever-after. But that was where the dreams had ended. Occasionally, Natty visualised life in her marital mansion, hosting glittering balls and sophisticated cocktail parties. But she'd never fantasised about the domestic side of life, much less motherhood.

Towards the end of their laughing, sticky, sun-drenched lunch, however, Natty was startled by how easily she'd slipped into the role of 'mum' alongside Matt's 'dad'.

She wasn't sure whether she was remembering the things her mum had said and done or whether they were coming to her instinctively, but she'd seldom felt more comfortable.

With Matt lying propped on one elbow beside her, and Rosie eating ice-cream on the sand in front of her crossed ankles, Natty dared to wonder if it would be as easy to be Rosie's stepmum full-time. Was it really possible to go from being a single twenty-one-year-old one minute to having an instant family the next, without pregnancy, childbirth or the baby stages?

Natty wondered how she would feel in the long term, knowing Rosie wasn't hers. Would Rosie be a constant reminder of Jen, the woman Matt had loved first? Would the child be a wedge between her and Matt?

Even as the question crossed Natty's mind, however, she was ashamed of it. As Jude had said of David's flowers, roses were roses — they were just as beautiful wherever they came from. So were children, Natty realised.

As Natty gazed lovingly at Rosie, she saw without registering a sudden mischievous look creep onto the girl's face.

She watched as Rosie dug her spoon into an ice-cream tub and gathered a big dollop of raspberry ripple. She gazed without suspicion as Rosie turned the spoon into a catapult, braced the handle with her right thumb and pulled back the big scoop of ice-cream and bright red syrup with her left hand.

How sweet the child looked, thought Natty, even as she saw the lump of sticky ice-cream come flying off the end of the spoon, heading her way.

The whack in the chest knocked Natty out of her reverie. The thump was followed by a freezing cold chill soaking through her white blouse.

She looked down in horror. Gloopy, melting ice cream laced with a spider's web of sticky red syrup seemed to cover her entire chest.

Natty went into shock.

My vintage blouse! she thought. *It's sixty years old! It's absolutely ruined!*

'Rosie!' Matt shouted in horror.

Rosie's lip began to wobble at the sound of her dad's sudden anger. But, to Matt's surprise, and to Natty's own surprise, Natty was suddenly laughing. She wasn't sure if it was hysteria or shock-induced lunacy, but she felt suddenly light-headed and completely carefree.

'Right, madam,' Natty said in a playful-cross tone, 'so that's how you want to play, is it?'

Natty dug a spoon into her ice cream and catapulted a dollop onto the front of Rosie's dress. Rosie laughed and catapulted another splodge at Natty.

Like an astonished tennis spectator,

Matt turned left and right as ice cream flew back and forth, faster and faster, and the two girls he loved most laughed louder and louder.

Eventually, Matt copped a slug of ice cream in the ear and called an end to the food fight. He tore some kitchen paper from a roll he'd brought with him and offered it to Natty. His face was full of apology on seeing the full extent of raspberry ripple goo covering Natty's blouse.

'I'm so sorry, Natty . . . ' Matt's tone was abject. 'Rosie's normally so good.'

'She is being good!' Natty wiped tears of laughter and smears of mascara from her eyes. 'I haven't enjoyed myself so much for years!'

'But your blouse! Your make-up!'

'It's only clothes and make-up,' Natty assured him with a smile. In a trilling soprano, she added, 'And I can't believe that I just said that!'

* * *

Natty repaired her make-up in the mirror of her compact. She got the worst of the ice-cream off her blouse, and the stains she couldn't get out she found she really didn't care about. Compared to being with Matt and Rosie, she realised that clothes really were just clothes. Even record deals and hit singles didn't seem to matter at that moment. As they walked along the glistening water's edge, the important things were the feel of Matt's hand in her right hand, and Rosie's in her left.

After an afternoon playing with Rosie on the seashore, Matt drove them back into town. They bought fish and chips from a shop on the busy prom and ate them on a wrought iron and wood bench overlooking the sea. Neither Natty nor Matt wanted to take Rosie home, but it was clear the child was growing tired and they reluctantly agreed they had to.

Matt strapped Rosie into the back seat of the car and she fell into a doze before he'd slid his muscular frame behind the steering wheel. From the passenger seat, Natty gazed lovingly at the cherub and blew her a little night-night kiss. She turned forward in her seat in time to find Matt gazing at her.

'I'm so glad you came today, Natty. You're so good with Rosie — she's really enjoyed herself.'

'She's so adorable,' said Natty warmly. 'I hope we can do it again very soon.'

In a quiet, almost fragile tone, Matt murmured, 'Be nice to make it permanent.'

'Perhaps we can,' agreed Natty.

'Maybe,' Matt answered wistfully.

'Maybe . . . ' Natty blurted. Guiltily, she glanced back to check she hadn't woken Rosie. But, really! Natty was astounded. The other night Matt had virtually proposed. He'd just done it again, hadn't he? And she'd virtually accepted. Surely that deserved a more emphatic response than 'maybe'?

It was lucky she was lost for words because before Natty could gather the breath to give him a piece of her mind, she noticed the sad way Matt had turned away, his nearest arm resting on the steering wheel as though he wanted to hide behind his big muscular bicep.

Her anger cooling to fear, Natty said, 'Matt, what's wrong?'

Matt shrugged his powerfully built shoulder. He avoided her eyes. Eventually, he let out a heavy sigh. Still not looking at her, he said, 'I'm sorry, Natty. I'm really pleased about your record deal, don't think I'm not. I suppose I'm just scared that it's going to take you away from me.'

Natty stared at him, open-mouthed. 'Of course it won't . . . '

'Like Gary said, there'll be recordings, meetings, tours. It won't leave much time for anything else.'

'You can come with me!' Natty blurted. 'Bring Rosie, too.'

Matt smiled weakly. 'It's not just that. Look at that house of Gary's and that Jag of Cameron's. That's the world you're moving into — and you deserve it, Natty. It suits you. You were born to be rich.'

'And that's a bad thing?' Natty said, confused.

'No, of course it's not. Until you look at me. I'm washed up, Natty. Let's face it, the ice-cream parlour will go to Jen. I've moved back in with my mum. I'm even down to driving my mum's car with a big pair of knickers on the side! What can I possibly offer a pop star?'

'But if I make it,' Natty reasoned, 'you won't need to earn any money!'

She gave him her brightest grin. Matt's downcast expression didn't flicker and as Natty gazed at it, her face began to fall, too. Even as she said it, Natty knew the prospect of her supporting Matt didn't feel right. A lifetime's diet of black and white romantic movies had left her in no doubt that it was supposed to be the girl who married the millionaire.

14

When Natty got home from work the following evening, Matt was standing at the top of the steps to the front door, grinning broadly and waving at her — in a rather over-the-top way, she couldn't help thinking.

'Er . . . Hi!' Natty waved back, somewhat puzzled. Matt kept waving and Natty realised why he was waving. Or, rather, *what* he was waving. The third finger of his left hand was ring-less.

'You had it cut off!' Natty threw her arms around him and pressed her cheek to his chest.

'Fire station, like you said,' Matt informed her. 'I nearly bottled out when I saw the saw! But it came off as good as gold. Well, it was gold! But come in, Cameron's already here.'

Natty hurried down the hall. In the

dining room, she found Margie chain-smoking and Jude and Jase looking equally anxious. Cameron was standing in front of the fireplace in a waistcoat and ribbon tie. The pale face below his jutting black quiff was as solemn as a funeral director's.

Natty's stomach was suddenly so full of butterflies she couldn't speak.

'For goodness sake spit it out!' Margie urged. 'I've already bitten my fingernails down to the elbows!'

Cameron's face was hard to read. 'There are still some details to work out, but we're looking at a million-pound deal . . . '

'A million!' Natty went from standing to sitting on the sofa as quickly as if a rug had been pulled from beneath her feet.

Cameron held up his palms like train buffers. 'Before you get too excited, when they say a million they're talking about the complete package: cost of recording, promotion, a couple of videos . . . In terms of cash up front, you're looking at around two hundred thousand.'

'Natty, that's amazing!' Margie squealed.

'Two hundred thousand!' Natty repeated the words in shock. To her, it might as well have been a million. With two hundred thousand she'd be able to buy anything! She could buy out Jen's share of the ice-cream parlour. That wouldn't be supporting Matt, would it? They'd be equal partners. She might even be able to put down a deposit on a home for the two of them.

Natty's mind was racing so far ahead that it took her a moment to realise Cameron was clearing his throat, awkwardly.

'There's just one wee snag,' the Scot said quietly. 'The label won't advance the money until Gary delivers the album.'

Natty, Matt, Jude, Jase and Margie exchanged uncertain glances, none of them understanding. Eventually, Margie ventured cautiously, 'That's not a problem, is it?'

Cameron eased a finger between his neck and shirt collar. 'Remember, we're talking about an album we want at least a million people to buy. That means the best studio, best musicians. I've talked to Gary long and hard about it. He reckons we can make it for about fifty grand.'

'We?' Natty squeaked.

Cameron looked embarrassed and murmured, 'Gary hasnae got the money.'

Natty burst out laughing, then realised there wasn't so much as the flicker of a smile playing on Cameron's lips. Feeling sick, she said, 'You are joking — aren't you?'

'I'm afraid not, Natty.'

'What about that house?' Matt protested. 'It must be worth several million!'

Cameron sucked his teeth. 'I'm afraid Gary has got a wee bit ahead of himself with that house. He bought it with a private loan from a big name in the business; it's how the big earners move some money out of the taxman's reach and newcomers like Gary get to enjoy royalties they won't get their hands on for a couple of years.

'Dinnae get me wrong,' Cameron said quickly. 'When the money comes through from the 3-Dom hits, Gary and the girls will be millionaires several times over. At the moment, the girls are on five hundred a week and Gary's on not much more. He spends more than that putting petrol in his Ferrari.'

'So he wants us to pay for the album?' Margie surmised.

Natty flopped on the sofa in despair. 'Where on earth could we get fifty thousand?'

Cameron looked around the stunned faces and said quietly, 'If Gary says he can make the album for fifty thousand, I reckon I can pull in some favours and make it for forty. I'm no' a wealthy man, but I can put in ten grand to make this work. If we all do the same we'll be there.'

'Count me out!' Jude put her hands in the air and swept from the room, saying breezily, 'I haven't got thirty pence.'

Natty glared after her. She knew Jude really was a penniless artist, but even so! Natty had expected some sisterly concern at the very least!

'Matt?' Cameron raised an enquiring eyebrow.

Matt reddened and looked away. 'I'd like to help, Natty, but the way things are at the moment with Jen . . . I could maybe scrape together a couple of grand, but that's about it.'

Matt looked wretched, and Natty saw his shame at being unable to offer more. She knew how much it meant to him to be a provider. Natty was filled with a surge of love for him, for offering what little he had, especially as he thought a record deal would take her away from him. Overwhelmed by his sacrifice, she got up from the sofa and hugged him where he sat at the dining table. She kissed his neck, gratefully.

'Sorry I can't be the big hero and pay for it all,' Matt muttered, glumly.

'You'll always be my hero,' Natty whispered in his ear.

In an increasingly desperate tone, Cameron said, 'Jason . . . ?'

Jase looked anguished, and Natty's heart went out to him, too. Natty knew Jase was as skint as the rest of them. Why else would he be renting a room in his forties?

But Margie couldn't bear to watch her adopted family squirm any longer.

'I'll put up the money!' she beamed. 'Thirty thousand, right? That's what you said.'

'And it's strictly short term,' Cameron assured her. 'You'll get it back twofold, in six months maximum.'

'Where are you going to get thirty thousand?' Matt asked his mother in disbelief.

'I'll borrow it!' Margie beamed. 'Against this place. It must be worth a fortune by now. I'm on good terms with my bank manager. If I say the money's for the shop he'll put it through on a handshake.'

Margie glanced at the clock. 'I'll call him at home now and write a cheque straight away.'

Cameron cleared his throat. 'Would cash be possible? It tends to make things cheaper in this business.'

Margie gave the Scot a level look, then said, 'Come round at seven tomorrow. I'll have the money waiting.'

★   ★   ★

'Thank you so much!' Natty threw her arms around Margie and planted a smacker on her cheek. 'You've made all my dreams come true!'

'Nonsense!' Margie hugged her. 'This is just a loan to make it work. You're the one who's landed a million-pound deal! This deserves a celebration. Get the glasses, Jase!'

'Your wish is my command, mistress!'

Margie put a Seventies disco compilation on the hi-fi and an impromptu party broke out.

Natty was light-headed. She was going to be a star! She and Matt would be rich. And it was all because of Margie, the best mother-in-law a girl could wish for! Natty could barely take it in.

As the others chatted excitedly, she noticed that Matt looked down and deflated. Natty slipped up behind him where he sat, wrapped her arms around him and propped her chin on his muscular shoulder.

'Fancy a drive down to the prom?' Natty whispered.

Matt smiled weakly. 'Only if you don't mind going out with a penniless loser.'

'Only if you can bear going out with a singing sensation,' Natty grinned back.

'And only if you don't mind going in Mum's car,' said Matt. 'Jen's got the Chevy again.'

They went out through the kitchen. Matt backed the Posh Knickers-mobile out of the yard and into the alley at the back.

As they drove down the high street, Natty said, 'When I get my advance I'll buy us a new Chevy — a Cadillac even! How about a fifty-nine convertible in candy-apple red to match my hair?'

Matt gave her a half-hearted chuckle and Natty trilled, 'Sorry! I'm not helping, am I?'

Matt drove past the bright lights of the prom. Towards the edge of the town he pulled into a bay facing over the beach and the sea.

'Congratulatory kiss for the singing sensation?' Natty asked. She posed her lips invitingly.

Matt cheered up and leaned towards her. 'Now this is something I can do . . .'

For the next twenty minutes, the only sounds were the moist whispers of two sets of lips becoming reacquainted. Eventually they both came up for air and flopped back contented in their respective seats, hands held tightly above the gear-stick.

'Now that's something money can't

buy!' Natty sighed.

'Good job there's something!' Matt grinned.

At length, Natty said, 'I know you feel funny about me making more money than you . . . but you'll just have to get over it! It won't be forever, anyway. You come from a family of businesspeople. You'll probably be the ice-cream king of England in a couple of years' time.'

'Don't you ever have any doubts about anything, Natty?'

She smiled to herself. *If only you knew!* she thought.

In the shadows of the car, she held his hand in both of hers and lovingly massaged the band of white flesh where his wedding ring had been. At length, she confessed, 'I did have my doubts about you and Jude.'

'*Jude?*' Matt exclaimed in disbelief. 'You thought that Jude and I were . . . '

'I know it sounds silly,' Natty admitted. 'But I did walk in on you having that big heart-to-heart the other week. What was that all about?'

Matt frowned, trying to remember. Eventually he said, 'Oh that. I was just asking her about her daughter, Carla. How she coped when Jude got divorced. You know, thinking about Rosie. Looking for some advice on how to do it, I guess.'

'It must be tough when there's a child involved,' Natty said, sympathetically. 'I know I'd feel guilty if it was me.'

In truth, Natty felt guilty just being involved with Matt while he was splitting up with Rosie's mother.

'It's not as if I haven't tried,' Matt said bitterly. 'But when the other person's in love with somebody else . . . '

'Somebody else?' Natty whispered, shocked.

Matt's face was in profile and in shadow. At length, he let out a pained sigh.

'Some clever-clogs doctor Jen met at university. I thought he was just a friend of hers. He went on to medical school and worked abroad for a while. Jen and I got married and I thought that was the end of it. But then you notice the letters, phone calls, texts . . .

'I confronted her, but it just made her secretive. Especially since he started working at the hospital down the road. She's always insisted they've never had an affair but whatever there is between them, it goes a lot deeper than anything she ever felt for me.'

'Oh, that's awful, Matt,' said Natty, her voice full of sympathy. She stroked his hand, comfortingly.

Matt shrugged. 'Looking back, I should have seen the signs before we married. I guess we were too young to know who we were and what we wanted from life. We'd been going out since we were at school and I just kind of assumed we'd get together. In a way I'm happy for her. We're both free now to be with someone we can truly love.'

He turned to look at her intensely. 'Can you see, though, why the thought of you going off to a life of fame and fortune scares me so much? What if you meet some pop star you've got more in common with?'

★　★　★

Cameron arrived the following evening on the dot of seven. In the centre of the dining table stood a pink and yellow bag with the Posh Knickers logo on the front and a picture of a black lace thong on the side. Inside the bag was £30,000 in neat bundles of twenties.

'Would you like to count it?' Margie asked.

Cameron's lips flickered but he held up a palm to show he trusted her. From a slim leather file, he produced a several-page document and put it on the table in front of Natty.

'One contract with Gary's production company. No need to sign it until you've had a lawyer look it over, but I've read it through and it's a standard form.'

Cameron produced another document from the file. 'I've also taken the liberty of drawing up a management contract. Now the deal with Gary is in writing, I hope you'll consider appointing me your manager.'

'I'd be delighted to, Mr Swoon!' Natty trilled. 'I still can't believe this is happening!'

'This deserves a toast!' Margie declared. 'Grab some glasses, Jase!'

'Will do,' he replied.

'Oh, where's Matt?' Margie fussed. 'He came home a minute ago.'

'I think he's upstairs doing something on the computer,' Jude said airily.

At that moment, the sound of Matt's crepe soles came bopping noisily down the stairs. Margie glugged champagne into some glasses. 'You'll stay for a drink, Cameron?'

Cameron slipped his left hand through the handles of the Posh Knickers bag and said, 'Just a quick one, then.'

Matt burst into the dining room, a piece of paper clutched in his hand. His face wore an expression Natty had never seen him wear before. Her stomach tensed and her heart began thumping as she realised something was badly wrong.

'Ah, Matt, there you are . . . ' Margie began.

Matt ignored his mother. He stared at Cameron, his chiselled face stony.

'I'm glad I caught you, Cameron,' Matt said in a hard tone. 'Perhaps you could explain this picture I've just downloaded from the internet.'

Matt slapped the sheet of paper on the dining table. The others gathered around to take a look. It was the photograph that had adorned the wall in Gary Morris's study — the producer surrounded by the girls from 3-Dom against the background of a tropical beach. Except there was something different . . .

'It's not him! It's not Gary!' Natty cried, startled.

'You're right!' said Jase. 'It's not!'

Natty stared at the picture, trying to work out what had happened. She wasn't a fan of modern technology. But even she reckoned it was probably easy with today's computers to superimpose a face from one photo onto another. She also had a sickening feeling that the picture on the table wasn't the one that had been doctored. They'd met an impostor!

'So who was the man we met?' Matt demanded of Cameron.

Natty felt as though the world was falling away from beneath her feet and taking all her dreams with it. They hadn't met Gary Morris. There was no million-pound deal. Cameron had tried to con them out of £30,000. Trembling, she searched Cameron's face for an explanation. His expression was as blank as ever, except for a small muscle beside his left eye which had begun to twitch nervously.

In a single movement, Cameron swung the Posh Knickers bag from the table and slammed his fist into Matt's stomach with a resounding crump!

'Matt!' Natty and Margie screamed in harmony.

Matt folded in half like a newspaper. Cameron shoved past him and made a break for the kitchen. As Matt crumpled to the floor, though, he grabbed the bottom edge of the Posh Knickers bag. The plastic ripped and bundles of twenty-pound notes flew out in every direction.

In the doorway to the hall, Cameron turned back and stared at the money scattered on the kitchen floor. For a split second he looked about to grab one of the bundles.

'No you don't!' said Matt, springing back to his feet.

Cameron turned on his heel and sprinted down the hall to the front door. Matt ran after him, his muscular arms pumping like pistons. Out of sight in the hall came the crack of a fist hitting a jaw.

'Matt!' Natty and Margie screamed again.

Natty ran to the hallway, the others hot on her heels. To her relief she found Matt breathing hard and rubbing the knuckles of his right fist. Lying flat on his back in his black drape suit, with his quiff pointing skyward, Cameron was out cold.

'My hero!' Natty exclaimed.

Matt grinned. 'I caught him with a lucky one!'

15

A week later, Natty was sitting behind the reception desk at the local newspaper, tapping away at a battered laptop. She wished it was a proper manual typewriter with big clattering keys, a bell that dinged at the end of each line and a carriage she could slam back with a satisfying screech. That would have made her feel like a real reporter. But even her traditionalist boss insisted they had to produce the paper with modern technology, the same as everyone else.

'Hi, Natty . . . Aaaaagh!' Matt burst through the door at a run. His crepe sole landed on one of the loose floor tiles. The tile flew out from beneath him and he crashed full-length to the dusty floor.

'Matt!' Natty ran out from behind the desk. She was wearing a knee-length check pencil skirt and tight pale blue roll-neck. She'd always liked the

Jane Russell 'sweater girl' look — demure, yet when worn with a bullet bra, likely to paralyse any man at fifty paces. Her ruby-red hair was pinned up like Audrey Hepburn to become the ultimate 1950s secretary.

She helped Matt to his feet. 'Are you all right?'

'I'm fine!' Matt said dizzily. 'Just nervous, I guess!'

'We'll have to do something about that!' Natty said. 'You're turning me into a nervous wreck!'

Natty went back behind the desk and Matt leaned over the top. 'What are you up to?' he asked.

'Ace reporter Natty Smalls is writing her first national exclusive!' Natty said proudly. 'My part in foiling the Great 3-Dom Swindle!'

'I hope I get a mention!' Matt grinned.

'Every story needs a hero!' she quipped. 'If it hadn't been for you, your mum would have lost her money and Cameron would still be out conning people.'

Natty slumped in her chair and let

out a heavy sigh. 'I still can't believe I didn't suspect Cameron was a crook.'

'You weren't the only one he fooled,' Matt reminded her.

After Cameron was arrested it emerged he owed his pallid complexion to being in and out of prison for deception and fraud ever since he left school. On his last sojourn behind bars he met another conman who did a convincing impersonation of Gary Morris.

The pair had worked the scam on hopeful singers in six cities up and down the country. The big house was owned by a businessman who had left it in the care of a house-sitting agent matching Cameron's description. The Jaguar was hired on a stolen credit card. Even the tailor who made Cameron's suits had gone unpaid.

'At least you saw through him,' said Natty. 'You didn't like Cameron from the start.'

'Something my dad taught me about business,' Matt said fondly. 'If something looks too good to be true, it probably is. I have to admit that when Cameron took us to that big house, he had me totally convinced. But when Mum was actually going to part with the cash, I guess some instinct kicked in and made me want to check him out.'

Natty gazed admiringly at Matt — he really was her hero.

'It's a shame, though, isn't it?' Natty sighed. 'I thought I was going to get a record contract. I thought we'd be rich.'

'And who says we won't be?'

Matt's teasing tone made Natty look up, curiously.

A blush rose to Matt's chiselled cheeks as he said excitedly, 'I didn't tell you before in case nothing came of it. But I got some names from Justin and Duke and sent copies of your demo and photos to some producers and record companies. And guess what? One of them just phoned me and said he really likes it!'

'No!' Natty slapped her palms to her cheeks as her mouth fell open.

'Don't get too excited!' Matt said

quickly. 'It's not a million-pound deal or anything like that — I guess in real life that takes a little more work. But he says if you get some experience over the next couple of years he can see you getting a record contract. In the meantime he wants to book you as a support act on a national tour — twenty dates ending up at the Albert Hall!'

Natty screamed. She threw her arms around Matt and kissed him full on the lips.

'I take it you're pleased!' Matt said, when she finally released him.

'Of course I am . . . ' Natty's beam became a frown. 'But . . . I thought you didn't want me to go away on tour.'

'I'm coming with you!' Matt grinned.

Natty stared at him, confused.

'I've decided to let Jen have my share of the ice-cream parlour in the divorce settlement,' Matt explained. 'I need a clean start, so I thought I could be your manager.'

'Well, that's assuming I have a career to manage!' Natty replied, nervously.

'Of course you will! You'll be the biggest star that ever lived. But if it doesn't work out, we'll start a new business together, maybe a vintage clothes shop. As long as we're together, I don't care what we do.'

'Me neither!' Natty hugged him and kissed him again.

'I'm glad you said that,' said Matt quietly. 'Because . . . well, I was going to save this until dinner tonight, but I can't wait a minute longer.'

From his pocket Matt pulled a small red, velvet-covered box. He opened it on the reception desk. Nestling in a bed of ivory silk was the most beautiful diamond ring Natty had ever seen.

'It's vintage,' explained Matt. 'From 1959.'

'It's beautiful!' Her lip trembling, Natty wiped a pool of mascara from the corner of her eye.

'I don't know how long it will take to sort out my divorce,' Matt gabbled. 'And I don't know where we'll live, apart from Mum's, or what we'll do for money. In fact, I can't think of a single reason why you'd want me! But as soon as I'm free, Natty Smalls, and if you'll have me, I'd be extremely honoured if you would be my wife. Will you marry me?'

'I'll have to think about it,' murmured Natty.

Matt was a little taken aback. 'Oh, erm, well . . . of course, I understand . . .' he stammered.

'Thought about it!' Natty cried. 'And the answer is yes!'

For what need did a vintage girl have for mansions, furs and Cadillacs when she'd found the most old-fashioned treasure of all — the love of the most wonderful man in the world?

★   ★   ★

Later that night they hugged and kissed on the landing outside Natty's room.

'Well,' Matt sighed, 'I guess this is where I say goodnight.'

'Not necessarily,' Natty whispered.

Reaching behind her, she opened her bedroom door.

Matt was confused. 'I thought you believed in waiting . . . '

'I do,' said Natty. 'But since it might take a while to make it official, how about we pretend we're married now?'

THE END

We do hope that you have enjoyed reading this large print book.

Did you know that all of our titles are available for purchase?

We publish a wide range of high quality large print books including:
**Romances, Mysteries, Classics
General Fiction
Non Fiction and Westerns**

Special interest titles available in large print are:
**The Little Oxford Dictionary
Music Book, Song Book
Hymn Book, Service Book**

Also available from us courtesy of Oxford University Press:
**Young Readers' Dictionary
(large print edition)
Young Readers' Thesaurus
(large print edition)**

For further information or a free brochure, please contact us at:
**Ulverscroft Large Print Books Ltd.,
The Green, Bradgate Road, Anstey,
Leicester, LE7 7FU, England.
Tel:** (00 44) **0116 236 4325**
Fax: (00 44) **0116 234 0205**

THE GIRL FROM YESTERDAY

Teresa Ashby

Robert Ashton and Kate Gibson are a month away from their wedding. However, Robert's ex-wife Caroline turns up from Australia with a teenage daughter, Karen, who Robert knew nothing about. Then, as Caroline and Robert spend time together, they still seem to have feelings for one another, despite the fact that Jim, back in Australia, has asked Caroline to marry him. Now, Robert and Caroline must decide whether their futures lie with each other — or with Kate and Jim.

LOVERS NEVER LIE

Gael Morrison

Stacia Roberts has always played it safe, yet, longing for adventure, she travels to Greece expecting sunshine and excitement — and gets more than she'd ever bargained for. When strangers try to kill her, she suspects her fellow traveller Andrew Moore might be the enemy — but is he really a friend? Andrew blames himself for his wife's death. Then he falls in love with Stacia, vowing to keep her safe, a difficult task when he discovers she's an international thief.